The shifters move into the autumn season with anticipation of upcoming celebrations and thankful for their family and friends around them. But of course, there is always something, or someone, to add a little spice to their lives.

The Autumn Feast anthology features six more shifter stories from some of eXtasy Books' top authors and follows the lives of those who have previously featured in Spring Fever and Winter Magic. Join them in tales where the fiery color of the leaves may not be the only heat of the season.

Autumn Feast
Copyright © 2018 Charlie Richards, Catherine Lievens, Lynn Michaels, Liza Kay, Deja Black, Suede Delray
ISBN: 978-1-4874-2565-4
Cover art by Angela Waters

Published by eXtasy Books Inc or
Devine Destinies, an imprint of eXtasy Books Inc

Look for us online at:
www.eXtasybooks.com or www.devinedestinies.com

Autumn Feast

By

Charlie Richards, Catherine Lievens, Lynn Michaels, Liza Kay, Deja Black, Suede Delray

Capturing Autumn's Airy Breeze
A Wolves of Stone Ridge Short Story

By

Charlie Richards

When an air dragon finishes his penance to the king, he can finally track down his mate . . . but he discovers he's not the only one looking for him.

Agnoroth knew Kristof Merrill was his mate the second he scented him. Letting him go after holding him in his arms, even for a brief second, had been beyond difficult. Staying away from him for almost eight months to complete his penance to the king was damn near torture. Now Agnoroth is free to find and woo Kristof. His human is understandably wary, considering the first time they'd met Agnoroth had helped kidnap Kristof's friend. Even with the mate-pull on his side, Kristof resists. Can Agnoroth make up for his lapse in judgment and earn his mate's trust?

Reader Advisory: This story follows events that happened in Melting his Fiery Heart, part of the Winter Magic anthology.

DEDICATION

I can smell autumn dancing in the breeze. The sweet chill of pumpkin and crisp sunburnt leaves.
~Unknown

CHAPTER ONE

A gnoroth knew he'd fucked up.
The story of my life.

The Fates had been laughing at him that day over eight months before. Agnoroth had met his mate—Kristof—the other half of his soul, while helping the fire dragon, Perentian, kidnap the man's friend. The friend—Riley—had been mated to another dragon named Dagskon. Perentian had claimed Dagskon had stolen a valuable gem from him. The plan had been to use Riley as a bargaining chip to get the gem back.

The plan hadn't worked, naturally.

Along the way, Agnoroth had run into his half-brother, Kazeem, who was also mated with one of Kristof's best friends. A human named Stefan. Kazeem had explained the truth of the matter—that Perentian had stolen the gem from the dragon king, and Dagskon had returned it to the king. Once he'd known the truth, Agnoroth had released Riley, but the damage was done.

Kidnapping a mate was a very serious crime.

Agnoroth had been fortunate. Since Kazeem had stood up for him, speaking on his behalf to the king, Agnoroth had been given a reduced sentence. For helping Perentian—even though it'd been under false pretenses and duress—Agnoroth had still served six months in the king's service as a gardener.

He knew Perentian had been put to death, but kidnapping a mate hadn't been his only crime. Fortunately, before the sentence had been carried out, Perentian had revealed where he'd hidden the crystal orb he'd stolen from him. That had

1

been the main reason Agnoroth had agreed to help the dragon. He'd wanted his gem back, so he'd been sympathetic to the fire dragon's desire.

Being an air dragon, Agnoroth hadn't minded the work. He'd used his magick to blow the leaves into piles instead of actually raking. His abilities also made it easy for him to throw gusts of wind at trees to knock off ripe fruit, then guide them into his basket.

While the chores were menial, Agnoroth had found he'd enjoyed them, making his six-month sentence fly by.

Agnoroth stared at the apartment building. "And now I'm here," he mumbled, rubbing the back of his neck. He hadn't revealed who Kristof was to him to anyone. "Time to see if he'll even talk to me."

Tipping his head back, Agnoroth enjoyed the cool autumn breeze caressing his cheeks. He thought about that moment when he'd had Kristof in his arms. Grabbing his mate to stop him from interfering with Perentian had been spine-tingling. The feel of the human's body, even through the thick winter clothes, had caused his dick to swell. A second later, realizing who Kristof was to him and how their first interaction was about to go, Agnoroth had damn near felt his heart break.

So much for making a good first impression, but I'll make him understand.

For the last several weeks, Agnoroth had been watching Kristof's movements. He knew his mate worked as a mechanic and used a motorcycle to commute. The sight of Kristof on his older model *Indian* always caused Agnoroth's blood to heat and his dick to thicken.

Watching from the park bench across the street from the apartments, Agnoroth waited. He glanced at his watch and saw the time was twenty after six. Anticipation began to surge through him.

If Kristof kept with his pattern, he would be home within the next few minutes.

Agnoroth hummed as the sound of Kristof's *Indian* reached his ears. Peering down the road, he watched as his mate appeared. The man's faded jeans molded to his body, showcasing his very fine ass and his long, muscular legs.

As his mouth watered, Agnoroth rose to his feet. He kept his focus on Kristof as he exited the park and headed to the crosswalk. As Agnoroth waited for the light to change, Kristof parked his motorcycle and took off his helmet.

The way Kristof's muscles flexed drew a groan from Agnoroth's throat. He reached down and adjusted his growing erection as he watched Kristof unhook his backpack from the back of the bike. The beep of the crosswalk signal registered, and Agnoroth started swiftly across the street.

By the time Agnoroth reached the other side, Kristof was already heading up his walk toward his apartment building. He continued at a leisurely pace, hoping to reach his mate's door a moment after he'd entered his home. Just before Kristof reached the stairs that led to his third-floor apartment, someone called Kristof's name.

Agnoroth slowed his steps as he watched a tall, muscular blond man jog the last couple of steps to reach Kristof's side. When Kristof turned his attention toward the man, a scowl curved his lips. Kristof's eyes narrowed, and his expression darkened as he took in the man who was an inch taller and just as broad.

"What do you want, Casey?" Kristof asked, stepping back when the man—Casey—tried to reach out and touch him.

Casey smiled widely as he swept his gaze over Kristof in what was clearly a hungry manner. "Aww, don't sound like that, Kristof," Casey all but purred in a deep rumble. "You've been avoiding my calls, so I had to come by." Once again, Casey stepped closer and reached for Kristof, resting his palm on his leather-jacket-covered arm. "I've missed you."

Kristof growled softly as he turned, pulling away. "I told

you we were through, Casey," he stated, his tone beyond cold. "Take off."

"You don't mean that," Casey cried, grabbing at his arm again.

"I do mean that," Kristof countered, half-turning to face him. "All I wanted was fidelity, and you couldn't give me that, so we're through."

Casey's lecherous expression disappeared as his eyes narrowed. His features took on a hard look. "You went away for two weeks without telling me. That wasn't my fault," he declared. "Besides, it was just a blowjob." Casey scoffed. "I don't even know how you found out about it in the first place."

"How I found out is beside the point," Kristof growled. "And I did tell you. Now, let go of me before I—"

"Before you what?" Casey demanded, his blue eyes flashing with anger. "You gonna hit me, Kris?" His lip curled as he leaned close. "You're not into that, *remember*? *I* am, and if you think for a second that you get to decide to walk away from me before I'm done with you, then—"

"Then you should listen to Kristof and walk away," Agnoroth declared, unable to stand by and watch his mate be manhandled. By the time he finished speaking, Agnoroth had reached their side. "Release him now."

Casey didn't obey. Instead, he pinned Agnoroth with a scathing look. "Keep walkin', fem," he ordered, sneering. "You don't wanna get involved in this."

Agnoroth ignored the insult—*fem*, short for effeminate. He'd heard it before. Due to the fact that he was an air dragon, his voice in human form came out a surprisingly high tenor. That didn't bother him.

What bothered him was the fact that Casey wasn't obeying.

Fighting back his desire to unleash his claws and tear into the asshole human, Agnoroth narrowed his eyes and hissed, "I'm already involved."

Kristof's gasp drew both men's attention. His mate's dark eyes appeared wide, betraying his shock. Even his face began to pale.

Damn. Not the reaction I was hoping for.

Oh, wait. That's a flush. And did he just glance toward my groin?

Nice!

"Hi, Kristof." Agnoroth did his best to keep his voice soothing and warm. "Sorry, I'm late."

"Agnoroth!"

Upon hearing Kristof whisper his name, a deep sense of satisfaction flooded Agnoroth.

He remembers me.

"You know this guy?" Casey snapped, reminding both men of his presence.

Agnoroth lifted his hand to Casey's shoulder and squeezed, carefully modulating his much-greater dragon's strength. "Yes, Casey. Kristof and I know each other." He pinned a glare on the man, letting just a little of his dragon through. "Let my boyfriend go, Casey."

Even as the stench of fear flooded the air, Casey gave Agnoroth a belligerent smile. "Your boyfriend?" He turned to focus on him, which meant he released Kristof. "He ain't yours, fem. He's mine. Has been for—"

"I dumped your ass at the beginning of the year, Casey," Kristof claimed. "I don't belong to anyone. I'm my own man." He pointed at Agnoroth, his dark eyes sparking. "That means I ain't yours, either."

Making a mental note to watch his use of possessives, Agnoroth dipped his head in acquiescence as he used his hold to shove Casey toward the grass. "My apologies, Kristof. I'll remember that."

Casey must have been surprised by the force of Agnoroth's shove, for his eyes widened. "This ain't over, Kristof," he declared, raising his hand and pointing at him.

5

Before either of them could respond, Casey spun and stalked away.

Agnoroth watched Casey until he disappeared around the corner, then turned his attention back to Kristof. Except, Kristof no longer stood there. Lifting his gaze, Agnoroth spotted his mate's third-floor apartment door clicking shut.

Shit.

CHAPTER TWO

Kristof slammed the door behind him and rested his back against it. A second later, he reached over and remembered to flick the lock. Blowing out a rough breath, he fought against the mix of arousal and guilt that surged through him in equal measure.

Grimacing, Kristof pressed the heel of his palm against his fly and the base of his throbbing erection.

Holy shit. I thought it was a fluke.

Kristof ruthlessly pushed that thought from his mind. Yanking his phone from his pocket, he wondered who he should call about Agnoroth's unexpected appearance. Even though the air dragon had gotten him out of a tight spot with his ex-boyfriend, Kristof couldn't imagine the male was there for a good reason.

Hell, the only time Kristof had met Agnoroth, the dragon had been helping another of his kind kidnap his buddy, Riley.

Kristof figured contacting Kazeem was the obvious choice. The water dragon—who specialized in manipulating ice— was Agnoroth's half-brother. The problem was, the dragon shifter who was mated to Kristof's good buddy, Stefan, lived hours away in Steamboat Springs.

The natural second was Benjamin Sturgis. The earth dragon was mated to another of Kristof's best buddies, Cory. The pair lived in Denver so could get there fast. Plus, Benji was a pretty down-to-earth guy, so he wouldn't overreact even as he came to aid him.

Ha! Earth dragon. Down-to-earth!

Ugh! Focus, dumb-ass.

Kristof's indecision cost him.

Soft tapping sounded on the other side of the door. "Kristof Merrill." Agnoroth's surprisingly high-pitched voice could still easily be heard. "Open the door, Kristoff."

Gasping at the way Agnoroth's sexy accented voice said his name, Kristof felt his stomach clench as need rushed through him.

Oh, fuck! Why do I love the sound of his voice?

"Kristof, you know that I could easily break this lock. Just open the door." After an instant, Agnoroth murmured, "I won't hurt you, Kristof. You have my word on my honor as a dragon."

Seeing as Kristof had no idea if that meant anything, Kristof murmured back, "Give me a minute, please." As he dialed Cory's number, he figured being polite would be the best way to get a few minutes leeway.

"I'm not leaving, Kristof," Agnoroth replied, his voice quiet. "Not until I have a chance to speak with you . . . in private and face to face."

That was sort of what Kristof was afraid of. He felt shame at his responses because he found the bigger, broader man sexy as fuck. Just hearing his voice caused his prick to stand up and beg for attention.

The problem was, Agnoroth was the enemy.

Wasn't he?

Then why did he help me?

"Hey, Kristof. Don't tell me you're begging off dinner," Cory greeted. "We've had this planned for weeks! Feasting at Chen's!"

Kristof winced.

Shit! How did I not remember our plan to over-eat at the Chinese buffet-style restaurant in celebration of Cory's promotion?

Hearing the soft knocking on the other side of the door, Kristof remembered.

"Stop knocking!" Kristof barked. "If you're really legit you'll let me verify it!"

Even as Kristof heard a soft chuckle coming from the other side of the door, he grumbled into the phone, "I didn't forget about our dinner, but I had an unexpected visitor. I need to talk to Benji. He around?"

"Oooo-kaaaay. Heading to Benji's office," Cory responded. "Who is it?"

"Agnoroth," Kristof replied, seeing no reason not to tell his buddy.

"Agnor . . . who is—Oh, shit!"

Cory's next cry of *Benji* was easily heard through the phone line, but Kristof knew it wasn't directed at him.

There were muffled voices, Cory obviously talking to Benji, then the dragon's deep voice filled Kristof's ear. "Is it true?" Benji asked gruffly. "Agnoroth is at your place?"

"Yeah," Kristof confirmed.

"I'm on my way."

"Benji, wait a sec," Kristof called, afraid Benji was going to disconnect the line. "I have a question."

"First, are you safe? Injured?"

Kristof rolled his eyes. "I'm not injured." Glancing over his shoulder as if he could see through the door, he nibbled his lower lip for a second. "As far as safe, Agnoroth claims he won't hurt me. Swears it on his honor as a dragon. Does that mean anything to your kind?"

"Damn," Benji muttered, sounding surprised. "Then he won't hurt you. In fact, he would probably protect you if the situation came up while in his presence."

Nodding absently, Kristof realized that the man had already done it.

Huh.

"Then I guess you don't need to come over," Kristof claimed, even as butterflies took flight in his belly. "He says he wants to talk to me."

"I'm still on my way," Benji stated. "Just because he won't hurt you or allow you to be hurt, doesn't mean him being there is a good thing."

"Okay. See you when you get here, then," Kristof replied. It wasn't as if he could stop the dragon shifter and his buddy from coming over. Knowing he should be grateful that the pair were willing to drop everything because he might be in danger, Kristof even remembered to say thanks before hanging up.

Taking a deep breath, Kristof turned and unlocked the door. He gripped the handle, and after another pause to gird up his courage, he opened the door. Sweeping his gaze over Agnoroth, Kristof felt his blood heat in his veins.

Agnoroth had his hands braced on either side of the door frame, having obviously been waiting patiently.

Kristof couldn't help but admire Agnoroth's long, white hair, pale blue eyes, and chiseled features. His pale green polo shirt and black leather pants molded to his body as if they'd been painted on. While his frame was lean and toned, Kristof knew that the dragon had plenty of hidden strength.

The image of being pinned to the wall and pounded into by the beautiful dragon flashed through Kristof's mind. His blood pooled south, causing his balls to tingle. His heart fluttered in his chest.

A low growl rumbled from Agnoroth, and Kristof snapped his attention back to his face. The dragon's blue eyes appeared to glow with the intensity of his stare.

"I can guess at what you're thinking, Kristof," Agnoroth murmured, his tenor a rumbling purr. "Say it, and I will do it." He glanced pointedly at Kristof's groin, where he knew his erection pressed blatantly against his fly. "It would be my deepest pleasure."

Kristof's mouth went dry as he listened to Agnoroth's voice. The melodious tenor somehow felt like a physical caress against his skin. The hairs on his neck stood on end, and he clenched his hands to keep from reaching out and touching.

Finally, Agnoroth's words registered. "Y—" Kristof swallowed hard, trying to get moisture to his throat. "You're hitting on me?"

Agnoroth chuckled roughly as he straightened from his stance, then took a step forward. "If you have to ask, I must not be doing it properly." When he rested his hands on Kristof's upper arms and urged him backward a step, goose bumps broke out on his skin. "I'm doing more than hitting on you, Kristof."

The way Agnoroth slid his hands up Kristof's arms to his shoulders, then slipped inside his jacket so he could knead lightly, sent a wash of tingles down his torso, and his nipples beaded.

Kristof's arousal made it difficult to think. He found himself staring at Agnoroth's lips, wondering what they would taste like. Would he ravish Kristof's mouth, taking and dominating? Or was his passion more of a slow burn? The move of Agnoroth's head, dipping toward his, jerked Kristof out of his lustful musings.

"Wait," Kristof gasped, yanking backward and pulling away. He lifted his hands. "We can't do this. You said you wanted to talk."

Agnoroth inhaled deeply as his eyes narrowed. Lowering his hands, he dipped his chin as he blew out his breath between pursed lips. Then he nodded once, as if coming to a decision, and returned his focus to Kristof's face.

"You're right. You deserve an explanation." Agnoroth turned and closed the still-open front door. When he focused on Kristof once more, lust still swam in his eyes, but the fire seemed to be banked. "And an apology."

Kristof cocked his head. "Apology?" The arousal must

have still been effecting his brain because he wasn't following.

Arching one white-blond eyebrow, Agnoroth nodded. "For the incident with your friend."

Right. Of course.

Nodding, Kristof beckoned as he led the way into his living room, removing his jacket and draping it over the back of a chair in the process. "Shouldn't you really be apologizing to Riley, then? He's the one you kidnapped." He licked his lips as he settled on the sofa, then added, "Or maybe Dagskon, seeing as Riley is his mate?"

"I'll get to them . . . eventually." Agnoroth sat beside him, close enough that their thighs touched, sending a thrill through Kristof. "*You* are more important."

"Important?" Kristof couldn't help parroting the word. "Why?"

Agnoroth lifted his left hand and crooked his fingers. Skimming the backs of his forefingers along Kristof's jawline, he curved his lips into a hungry smile. "Because you, Kristof, are my mate."

"I-I'm—" Kristof leaped to his feet and faced the dragon. "Did you just say I'm your mate?"

Nodding, Agnoroth lifted his hand and beckoned. "Please sit back down. Please."

Kristof felt his knees buckle, his body forcing him to do as Agnoroth urged, and he sank back onto the sofa. He struggled to wrap his mind around what the male was telling him. His gut clenched as he thought about the dreams he'd had of the man and the many jerk-off sessions where the dragon's features swam through his mind.

Not to mention the guilt . . . and now it all makes sense.

Except.

"That was at Christmas last year. That was over eight months ago."

When each of his friends had met their dragon mate, the shifter had pursued them with single-minded dedication until they'd bonded. It had happened fast, too . . . normally within a few days.

"It's September. I met you at the beginning of winter, and now it's autumn! Where the hell have you been for almost nine months?"

CHAPTER THREE

Upon hearing Kristof's question, Agnoroth fought back a flinch. There was confusion in his mate's tone . . . and something else, too.

Hurt.

Agnoroth had ached to return to Kristof, the need a physical thing. On a daily basis, he'd had to fight his dragon. Only reminding himself that he would be put to death if he didn't complete his penance had kept him in control.

It hadn't occurred to Agnoroth that his human would be feeling the same pull, even if it was to a lesser extent.

"I'm so sorry I couldn't come sooner, Kristof," Agnoroth murmured, reaching out to him. When his mate cringed away from him, a stab of pain cut through him. "We only met for a moment in the woods."

That brief encounter where Agnoroth had wrapped his arms around Kristof, holding him still while Perentian had issued his ultimatum, had fueled so many fantasies.

"I wish things had been different when we met, but I can't change the past," Agnoroth told Kristof, lowering his hands to his lap. "Perentian had stolen something from me. Something I valued greatly, and he agreed to give it back to me if I helped him get his own gem back." Scoffing, Agnoroth shook his head as he eyed Kristof solemnly. "Even thinking back on it, I'm not sorry I did it."

Kristof scowled. "You're not sorry you helped an asshole kidnap my friend?"

Put like that . . .

Agnoroth shrugged. "No." Needing to touch, to have some contact, he tried again. As he slid his fingertips up Kristof's thigh, he murmured, "No, Kristof, because it brought me to you."

To Agnoroth's pleasure, Kristof didn't pull away. Instead, he glanced from Agnoroth's hand to his face and back again before lightly resting his own hand over Agnoroth's. On reflex, he tightened his grip before relaxing again.

Kristof's focus still appeared to be on their hands, but Agnoroth noticed how he kept giving his face side-long glances. His focus never seemed to make it to his eyes, however. As a few quiet minutes slipped by, Agnoroth couldn't resist gently kneading the hard muscle of his mate's thigh.

Finally, Kristof murmured, "You still didn't tell me where you were."

Agnoroth could scent Kristof's pain, frustration, and even a little anger and need. His mate had *needed*, but he hadn't understood why. The possibility hadn't occurred to Agnoroth, but even if it had, he didn't think he could have done anything about it.

So, to make him understand now . . .

"My half-brother is Kazeem. Did anyone tell you that?" Agnoroth began.

After Kristof had nodded, he explained everything. He shared how he'd been in a cell for a couple of weeks pending the king's decision. His penance had been six months manual labor as a gardener, and he told how he'd found he enjoyed the work. Then he'd come looking for his mate, but it had taken him a little while to find him.

"You've been following me for several weeks?" Kristof whispered incredulously. His eyes grew wide. "How did I not know that? And why wait so long?"

Agnoroth chuckled roughly. "I admit I struggled with how to approach you," he shared, fighting against the heat he felt creeping up his neck.

To Kristof's pleasure, his admission seemed to relax his mate. His human grinned as he waggled his brows. "Good to know a dragon can succumb to nerves, too."

Losing the fight against his blush, Agnoroth knew his cheeks were pink. Before he could come up with a response, the chime of the doorbell rang through the room.

Agnoroth growled. "If it's that asshole again, I'm going to wring his neck," he declared as he released Kristof and jumped to his feet. "Does Casey bother you often?"

"That should be Benji," Kristof told him, following. "He's the one I called."

Squelching his growl took nearly all Agnoroth's self-control. The fact that his mate called another dragon shifter for support rankled every damn one of his nerves. It didn't matter that it was an irrational feeling.

His mate was doing what he thought was necessary for his safety.

A good policy to have.

A fucking earth dragon, though. Gods, I hate them.

An earth dragon was a pain in the butt for an air dragon to fight and counter. Probably similar to how difficult it was for a water dragon to fight a fire dragon. Their specialties were opposites. That made the fight a test of strength of will, creativity, and guile.

If it wasn't to the death, the fight would be fun, all things considered.

When Agnoroth yanked open the door and spotted Benji, recognition hit. "Fuck!" he snarled gruffly. "I know you."

"And I you," Benji declared, stepping over the threshold without an invitation. The earth dragon's gaze slid past Agnoroth's shoulder. "Kristof? Are you okay?"

Agnoroth took a step back and to the side, allowing him to turn and keep both the other dragon and his mate in his sights.

Kristof nodded, his expression sheepish. "Yeah. I'm okay."

Growling upon seeing the way Benji peered intensely at Kristof—as well as how his nostrils flared, obviously scenting him—Agnoroth stepped close to his mate and wrapped his arm around him. To his pleasure, Kristof sank into his side.

An auburn-haired, hazel-eyed human pushed past Benji while saying, "Out of the doorway, hot stuff." The human glanced between Kristof and Agnoroth, then dismissing him, went to Kristof. "Tell me what the hell is going on, Kris. You okay?"

Agnoroth continued to growl low in his throat, but he didn't make a move to stop the human as he grabbed Kristof's upper arm, invading his space. Clenching his jaw, he reminded himself that these were his mate's friends and allies. They were there to help him . . . even though Kristof didn't need help to be safe from Agnoroth.

These men don't know that.

"Yeah, yeah. I'm okay," Kristof assured, patting the other human's hand.

Since Benji stood before him with his arms crossed and a glower on his face, Agnoroth assumed the human was Kristof's friend, Cory. The pair had been mated for almost a year and a half. It was through Benji's courtship of Cory that his own mate had learned that dragons existed.

Lucky turn of chance, that.

"Relax," Kristof urged, lifting his hands in placation as he glanced between everyone. "Agnoroth isn't here to hurt me." As he watched, Kristof sucked in a deep breath, as if he was stealing himself up to say something tough or controversial. After blowing out that same breath, Kristof waved Agnoroth's way as he stated, "Agnoroth is my mate. I've been dreaming about him for months. I—" His cheeks turned a deep red hue as he rubbed the back of his neck. Then he heaved a sigh as he flicked his gaze Benji's way. "You all don't lie about that kind of thing, right?"

Agnoroth felt Benji's hard gaze pinned on him. "No," he

muttered, his voice hard. "We don't." Then his eyes narrowed. "Do we?"

Knowing exactly what Benji was implying—or searching for, perhaps—Agnoroth tipped his head just a little as he held the other dragon's gaze. "No, we certainly do not lie about that kind of thing."

Even though Agnoroth understood why Kristof turned to Benji for confirmation, that didn't mean he had to like it. Pushing his annoyance down deep, he smiled at his human. He loved hearing Kristof's easy acceptance of being his mate.

"Well, I guess you'll be missing our Chinese buffet feast with us after all," Cory stated, a cheeky smile on his face.

Kristof cocked his head. "Huh? Why do you say that?"

Cory laughed as he eased away from his friend and was immediately wrapped up by Benji's open arms. "Because you two can't stop staring at each other." He winked when Kristof jerked his focus from where he and Agnoroth had been peering at each other to focus on him. "I couldn't even go a couple of days without giving in to my need for Benji. I can't imagine having waited for over eight months." Waving his hand imperiously, Cory stated, "Go fuck. Bond. Have fun." He winked. "We'll enjoy Chinese another time."

Growling softly, Agnoroth returned his focus to Kristof, wondering how he would take his friend's words. His mate's face was a dark hue, but he gamely crossed his arms over his chest and tipped his chin up, peering down his nose at Cory.

"Not like I haven't walked out of your house a time or two when you and Benji started going at it," Kristof commented dryly. "So don't give me shit about staring at a hot man."

"He's not giving you shit, are you, Cory?" Benji quickly countered, pulling his mate toward the door. Then he turned his attention to Agnoroth. "Congratulations."

Agnoroth tipped his head to the side as he felt his brows shoot up. "That's it?" Upon seeing the questioning look in

Benji's eyes, he added, "You rush over here to check on Kristof, then leave just that fast?"

Benji scoffed as he nodded. "You're mates. This is something you have to work out between yourselves." He glanced Kristof's way, his meaning clear, then he started him and Cory toward the door once more. "Holler if you need anything."

"Like more lube or something!" Cory cried even as Benji closed the door behind them.

Agnoroth flipped the lock, then focused on Kristof.

Kristof shrugged. "They're good friends."

Nodding, Agnoroth slowly began stalking toward his mate. "It's always good to have friends," he purred as he swept his gaze over the man. "But I'm just as glad that they're gone."

CHAPTER FOUR

Kristof swallowed . . . hard. The lust blazing in Agnoroth's eyes was unmistakable. He knew what the dragon shifter wanted to do. In truth, his body's arousal urged him to do the same.

But at what cost?

"I know nothing about you," Kristof stated on a pant while forcing his body back a step when Agnoroth advanced.

Agnoroth reached out and grabbed his hand, staying his retreat. "I will tell you anything you want to know about me," he offered while tugging Kristof closer. "It will always be the truth."

"How old are you?"

Geez. Why did I ask that? As if it matters.

Kristof knew dragons lived for centuries.

"I do not know my exact birthdate, but I have seen four hundred and thirty-three summers," Agnoroth immediately replied. "I was born in what is now considered Mongolia and still have a lair in the wilds there. It is an amazing place to dance on the wind."

Tensing, Kristof asked, "Do you expect me to move there?"

"No." Agnoroth slid his free hand around Kristof's back, rubbing along his spine. "Visit occasionally, but not live," he told him, trapping Kristof's hand against his chest.

Kristof felt the strong frame under his palm, and goose bumps erupted up his arm. His chest felt firm, and Kristof wanted to see what was hidden under the pale green polo shirt he wore. The rush of desire to tear the man's clothes from him nearly took his breath away.

"I-I'm having a hard time concentrating," Kristof admitted roughly, his blood rushing through his veins. "Why is that?" He shook his head, desperately trying to get his racing hormones under control. "Is it always like this?"

How had his buddy, Stefan, walked away from Kazeem for two weeks with feelings like these?

"We met over eight months ago, Kristof." Agnoroth tipped his head and nuzzled his temple against Kristof's own. "While we will always desire each other, that time apart has ramped up our needs. Our pull to mate is a whirlwind driving our arousal high, sweeping us away on an airy breeze."

Agnoroth's husky voice caused Kristof's skin to flush, and his nipples beaded. The way his breath ghosted over his skin caused the hairs on his nape to stand on end. His body trembled as Agnoroth wrapped his second arm around him and grabbed his ass, massaging lightly.

"I know most of your friends are here," Agnoroth rumbled as he began licking and nipping at the side of Kristof's neck. "So if here is where you want to stay, here is where we will be."

Kristof began to open his mouth to respond even though his brain was struggling to come up with a response.

"For a while, at least."

Cocking his head, Kristof pulled back a little. "What do you mean?" he asked, concern filling him.

Agnoroth met his gaze and swept his focus over Kristof's face. "Once we bond, you won't age, so in a decade, give or take, we would *have* to move."

Understanding flooded Kristof, and he nodded. "Right."

As his friends had met and bonded with other dragons, that was something he'd struggled with. His friends moving on without him. To his pleasure, he realized Fate wasn't going to be so unkind.

Kristof slid his hands over Agnoroth's chest, flicking his

soon-to-be lover's nipples through the fabric. "Let's do this, then."

"Are you certain?" Agnoroth asked while a hungry growl rumbled from him. His blue eyes blazed with need as he added, "I want you desperately, but it cannot be undone."

"I know." Kristof slid his hands up and gripped Agnoroth's nape, massaging lightly as he grinned up at him. "I never stopped thinking about you, even though—" He paused, blowing out a breath.

Agnoroth's smile turned understanding. "I get it. I was the bad guy."

"You were the bad guy," Kristof confirmed. Reconciling the truth would still take time, but he could do that later . . . when he wasn't thinking with his dick. Doing his best to express his thoughts, Kristof simply stated, "But you weren't really."

A wide smile curved Agnoroth's lips, telling Kristof he had said something right.

"Come with me," Kristof urged, slipping from Agnoroth's grip. At the same time, he grabbed the other man's hand.

To Kristof's pleasure, Agnoroth instantly obeyed, allowing him to draw him behind him.

Kristof's anticipation ramped up as he pushed open his bedroom door. Seeing his unmade bed and the jeans he had tossed over the back of the bench chest at the foot of his bed, he winced. He also had a towel left on the floor from when he'd showered last night.

Oops!

Giving Agnoroth a side-eyed look, Kristof tried to decide how the dragon was taking his general untidiness. He didn't consider himself a slob, but putting laundry away was rarely a priority. There was always something else to do.

Except, Kristof found that Agnoroth was eyeing the bed with a feral look of intent. Before Kristof could comment on it, his soon-to-be lover turned to him and gave him a wide grin. Then Agnoroth grabbed Kristof around his waist and tossed him on the bed.

Kristof bounced once, spreading his limbs for balance. Unable to help himself, he grinned. He couldn't even remember when he'd had a lover that could do that. His dick even twitched behind his fly at the feel of being tossed around.

Huh. Weird.

Agnoroth's nostrils flared, and his eyes narrowed. "Mmmm . . . got a fetish I should know about?" As he spoke, he stalked around the bed while yanking his polo over his head and tossing it to the bench.

Swallowing hard, Kristof watched as Agnoroth started on his jeans next. "M-Maybe," he forced himself to admit. There was no point in playing coy. "Never been with anyone who could toss me around like you just did. Kinda like it." Sucking in a harsh breath as Agnoroth shoved his jeans down and off, baring him to Kristof. "Oh, fuck," he whispered, riveting his focus on the dragon's long, *long*, slender prick. "Something else I like."

Kristof licked his lips as his chute muscles clenched. The guy had to be a foot if he was an inch. His erection would sink so deep inside him.

He couldn't wait.

Growling, Agnoroth grinned broadly as he winked. He reached down and gripped his erection. As he slowly jacked himself, he swept his gaze over Kristof.

"If you wish those clothes to stay intact, you should take them off," Agnoroth warned, offering him a shark-like smile. "Been apart too long, my mate, and I'm hanging on by a thread."

Kristof couldn't remember the last time someone had stared at him with such need in his eyes. His heart thundered in his chest as he lifted his arms and folded his hands under his head. Spreading his legs a little, Kristof gave the dragon a cheeky grin.

Another rumbling growl erupted from Agnoroth as his eyes flashed. For an instant, his pupils shifted to vertical, and Kristof felt his heart skip a beat. Then Agnoroth blinked, his eyes returning to normal, and he turned his attention to the nightstand.

Kristof watched as the dragon pulled out his tube of lube and tossed it onto the bed near his arm. Then Agnoroth climbed onto the bed and settled on his knees between Kristof's feet. Gripping each boot in turn, he pulled them off, followed by his socks.

Agnoroth grinned widely at Kristof. He leaned forward, resting his weight on his left hand and held up his other. "Don't move, my mate," he warned gruffly.

Then . . . his hand changed.

The fair skin of his hand and wrist paled as scales that appeared almost iridescent coated his skin. His fingers curled. From his fingertips grew long, white, lethal-looking claws.

When Agnoroth rested his claws on his stomach, Kristof sucked in a harsh breath.

"Relax," Agnoroth crooned. "You are safe."

"I-I know," Kristof immediately replied. Yanking his gaze from the dragon claw on his body, he met Agnoroth's pale blue eyes. "Ravish me."

Agnoroth grinned broadly, showing slightly sharper than normal teeth. "Gladly."

Then the sound of tearing fabric filled the room as Agnoroth rent Kristof's clothes from his body. The sight of his new lover's claws scraping over his skin combined with the light feel of their tips moving across his flesh. Kristof's breathing sped up as tingles erupted over every inch of his skin, right down to his toes.

By the time his clothes lay in tatters around his body, Kristof nearly levitated off the bed, his body felt such need.

With his cock throbbing and twitching, tapping and

leaking against his abdominals, Kristof whimpered, "A-Ag-noroth, please!"

Agnoroth grabbed the lube as his hand changed back to normal. "Gladly."

Chapter Five

Never in his wildest dreams had Agnoroth thought his mate would beg so beautifully. The way Kristof responded to his touch, how he moved and shuddered, enflamed his blood. His dick ached with his need as he poured a large dollop of lube onto his fingers.

"Roll over," Agnoroth demanded. As much as he wanted to see Kristof's face while ravishing him, he knew his control was damn near shot. Mounting his mate would be easier for their first time together, especially with his length.

"Hell yeah." Kristof swiftly obeyed, lifting his legs and turning. He drew his knees under him as he spread them, resting his weight on his elbows and arching his body. "Take me. God, I need you to pound my ass so bad."

Pleased at his mate's enthusiasm and acceptance, Agnoroth gripped Kristof's ass cheek and gently pulled it away from the other. He teased his slicked finger over his human's star, causing the man to twitch in his hold. When he pressed lightly, Kristof attempted to push back against him, obviously trying to hurry him along.

Seeing no reason to tease, Agnoroth quickly shoved his long finger deep into Kristof's chute. He held it there a few heartbeats, then pulled it free before repeating the move. Quickly working up to two, then three, Agnoroth reveled in the noises pouring from Kristof's mouth.

"Gods of the sky, the noises you make," Agnoroth muttered as he eased his fingers out of his mate. Gripping his dick, he slathered himself with the rest of the lube. "Gonna take you and make you scream."

Agnoroth sucked in a harsh gasp, the feel of his hand on himself and the gorgeous view before him causing the blood in his balls to boil. Moaning, he gripped the base of his prick and squeezed . . . hard.

At the same time, Agnoroth guided his crown to Kristof's stretched star.

"Now, now, now," Kristof chanted, somehow managing to cant his hips even higher in invitation.

Unable to wait an instant longer, Agnoroth pushed. His groan of pleasure upon feeling the tight clamp on his flared head nearly drowned out Kristof's moan. Rubbing up and down Kristof's spine with one hand, he gripped his lover's hip with his other.

Then Agnoroth sank deep, deep into his forever mate.

Agnoroth's heart soared as Kristof's hot, willing body enveloped him. His pulse rushed through him, making spots dance before his vision. Even his hands trembled with his need to rut.

Once Agnoroth had his groin pressed flush to Kristof's body, he levered over his mate. He rested his weight on his left hand as he wrapped his right arm around his man's waist and rubbed over his ripped abdominals. Nibbling at Kristof's tendon, Agnoroth relished the feel of coming together for the first time.

"God, Ag," Kristof muttered, turning his head and offering him more room. "You reach so deep. Damn!"

"Want to stay here forever." Agnoroth felt as if the words were ripped from him, but he wouldn't deny them. He couldn't. "My mate," he whined, licking up Kristof's neck.

Kristof moaned, his chute muscles rippling along Agnoroth's length. "Need you to fuck me, Ag."

Agnoroth growled, only too happy to obey. "Would do anything for you, Kristof, my mate, my forever." As soon as his crown tugged at his mate's ring, he changed direction.

Over and over, Agnoroth sank into Kristof. The slapping of skin filled the room as he reamed his lover's channel. The noises combined with the grunts, groans, and harsh breaths as both men moved together.

Feeling his balls tingle and tighten, Agnoroth growled low in his throat. His mouth watered as his orgasm threatened to overwhelm him. Needing his mate right there with him, Agnoroth slid his right hand down and gripped Kristof's thick cock. He rubbed his palm over the leaking slit, using his man's pre-cum to slick his palm, then he began jacking him in time with his thrusts.

Kristof bellowed his enjoyment, jolting in Agnoroth's hold. Then his mate shuddered and whined, his dick throbbing in his grip. He felt the heat of seed hit his hand as his mate's chute muscles rippled along his length.

Agnoroth's release swelled through him. His stomach clenched, and his heart pounded. His balls tightened as his cock pulsed, shooting stream after stream of seed deep into his mate's willing body.

Age-old instinct slammed into Agnoroth. Opening his mouth, he clamped his jaws on Kristof's shoulder. He struck, sinking his teeth into his mate's flesh.

Kristof's sweet, iron-rich blood welled up around his teeth. He sucked on the wound, searching for more of his human's life-giving nectar. As he swallowed another mouthful, Kristof's sweet scream of pleasure echoed through the bedroom.

Agnoroth slowly came back to himself, a low purr of contentment rumbling from him. After easing his teeth from Kristof, he licked over the wound. As he lapped up the last few traces of his mate's blood, his saliva sealed the mark.

Smug possessiveness flooded Agnoroth upon seeing his mark upon Kristof.

"Beautiful," Agnoroth muttered as he rubbed his nose

along it.

Chuckling huskily, Kristof turned his head and met his gaze. He smirked at him. "Me, my ass, or your mark?"

Agnoroth winked before pecking a kiss to Kristof's lips. "All three."

Then Agnoroth moved his hand from Kristof's softening prick to his lover's abdominals. He used the hold to ease them to the left. Once they were on their sides, he remained spooned up behind Kristof with his prick still cradled within him.

Kristof hummed as he clenched his chute muscles.

Groaning, Agnoroth nipped at his earlobe. "If you keep doing that, I'm going to fuck you again," he warned. His prick twitched within the confines of his lover's body.

Chuckling softly, Kristof met Agnoroth's gaze with a cheeky smile of his own. "Well, your dick is still hard in my ass, so what else should I expect you to do?"

Agnoroth moaned, tightening his arms around Kristof. "Gods of the sky, I want to empty my balls into you over and over." Licking a stripe up Kristof's neck, he added, "Love having you smell like me. Been waiting so long."

Kristof swallowed hard enough to cause his Adam's apple to bob . . . which drew Agnoroth's attention. Unable to help himself, he leaned forward and nipped at the slight bulge. To his pleasure, Kristof craned his neck and gave him more access.

Growling with his pleasure, Agnoroth began to suckle and lick between nips. "Gonna mark you here," he warned. "That okay?" At the same time, he began rubbing his right hand up and down his mate's chest, teasing over the ridges of his abdominals.

Heaving a deep groan, Kristof mumbled, "Hell yeah. Talking's overrated. Mark me."

Agnoroth was more than on board with that, and he

levered up on his left elbow. He gripped Kristof's right thigh and pushed it forward. To his delight, his mate grabbed a pillow and shoved it under his knee, lifting his leg and opening him further.

Having waited so damn long, Agnoroth's good intentions were swept away as if by an autumn breeze . . . and he began rutting into Kristof once more.

CHAPTER SIX

Kristof clenched his chute muscles as he drove his motorcycle toward home. As much as he loved feeling the residual traces of Agnoroth's dick in his ass, he could have done without the ribbing the guys at the shop had given him. His dragon hadn't been kidding when he'd said he was marking him.

Fucking hickey on my throat.

Even as he thought that, Kristof smiled. He sure had loved the way Agnoroth had given them to him. The dragon was a damn machine.

Agnoroth had fucked him through the mattress several times, finally sending Kristof into unconsciousness. His dragon had then woken him with a blowjob, followed by dinner in bed. Realizing that he'd made him miss a Chinese feast at a buffet restaurant, Agnoroth had ordered more take-out than he'd ever seen outside a restaurant—a veritable feast. He'd hand-fed him sweet and sour pork, pot stickers, and egg rolls. Then Agnoroth had made slow sweet love to him.

Kristof couldn't remember the last time he'd been so thoroughly taken care of.

And that's why he can leave as many marks on my body as he wants.

He grinned at his thoughts as he stopped his motorcycle at the light. So happy reliving his evening with Agnoroth, he only absently noticed the van pulling up beside him. The pain to the back of his head sent him and his motorcycle crashing to the ground.

Glaring upward, Kristof focused on Casey. "What the fuck, man?"

Casey smirked as he crouched beside him. "Where's your protector now?" He didn't give Kristof a chance to answer.

When Casey slammed his fist into Kristof's face again, it was lights out.

Kristof slowly swam to consciousness. His head pounded, and his jaw hurt like hell. Blinking blearily, he tried to take in his surroundings.

When Kristof attempted to bring his hand to his face to rub his eyes, he found he couldn't. That caused him to focus damn fast. Tipping his head back, he found his wrists tied to either side of him . . . and he was on a bed.

Oh, and my fucking legs are tied, too!

"What the fuck?"

"Ah, so you've finally woken." Casey came into view, and Kristof suddenly recalled what had happened on his way home from work.

"What the hell is this, Casey?" Kristof snarled, glaring at the man. He jerked his arms, feeling the ropes squeeze his wrists. There wasn't much play. "Untie me."

Casey laughed, his blue eyes gleaming with a crazed light Kristof hadn't seen in them before. "You're not in any position to demand anything," he stated, crossing his arms over his chest. Then his eyes narrowed as he focused on the marks on Kristof's neck. "Do you have any idea how pissed I am that you're wearing another man's marks when you're mine?"

Kristof did his best to keep his concern . . . and anger . . . out of his voice. "Casey, we broke up right after New Year's." *How many times do I have to repeat myself before the asshole gets it?* "It's time to move on." Tugging on the ropes again, Kristof kept his voice modulated as he again ordered, "Untie me, and I'll forget this ever happened." Another thought occurred to him. "And where's my bike?"

Uncrossing his arms, Casey reached behind himself. He pulled out a pair of large shears. After snapping them a few times, he leveled a wide, crazed-looking grin at Kristof's body.

"I'm glad you woke. I was getting tired of waiting." With his free hand, Casey palmed his crotch, drawing Kristof's attention to his boner. "I wanted you to be awake for everything, after all."

Shit!

Casey gripped the hem of Kristof's t-shirt and began cutting. The cold of the scissors caused a shiver to work through him. His gut clenched, and he tried to twist away.

Unfortunately, the ropes were too tight, and Kristof couldn't go anywhere. Casey actually started chuckling. That response ratcheted up Kristof's anger, sending it soaring.

Kristof sneered. "Is this really what you plan?" Seeing Casey's lips twitch and the way he barely paused at his words, his anger burned hotter through him. "You won't get away with this."

Snorting, Casey rolled his eyes. "How is that?" He finally deigned to answer Kristof's questions. "I took you on a corner with no traffic cameras and not like anyone saw. No one knows where we are." Casey returned to cutting off Kristof's shirt. "I'm gonna fuck your tight ass until you're a dried-up husk and I'm thoroughly through with you." Pausing in his ministrations, Casey once again cupped himself. "Can't wait to feel you bare. Can't wait to soak your channel with my seed. Always wanted to fill your hot body."

His nostrils flaring, a feral growl ripped from Kristof's throat. Anger and disgust surged through him. He leveled a hateful stare Casey's way.

"You do that, and there will be no corner of the earth you will be able to hide," Kristof vowed.

Casey laughed even as a dark specter moved across his blue eyes. "Yeah? Who's gonna stop me?" He finally spread

Kristof's shirt, baring his chest. As he rubbed his palm all over Kristof's chest, Casey purred, "I'll be satisfied, and you'll be dead."

"Not me," Kristof stated, praying his faith was well-founded. "I'm talking about Agnoroth."

Kristof smirked, his lips curling in disgust. "The fem? Seriously?" He rolled his eyes. "Whatever. That skinny little—"

A roar sounded through the air, rattling the windows . . . and Kristof grinned. "Oh, you're in the shit now, Casey." He snickered as he leveled a sneering gaze on his ex-lover. "You just bit off far, far more than you can chew. Big. Mistake."

Casey straightened as he glanced around, obviously listening as another roar swirled around the area.

To Kristof, the noise sounded like a cross between an animal's roar—a massive animal, dragon maybe—and the angry, shrill cries of the autumn wind. His heart quickened at the noise, and his pulse spiked. But it wasn't in trepidation—it was in anticipation.

That's my lover.

Just as the noise stopped rattling the window-panes, a crazy breeze swept through the enclosed loft space. It ruffled Kristof's hair and caressed his exposed skin. Instead of chilling him, it warmed him and even turned him on.

Holy shit!

"Agnoroth," Kristof gasped, his blood flooding his groin and causing his prick to lengthen.

"What the hell?" Casey whispered, staring around wide-eyed.

"Meet my lover." Kristof grinned widely, smug satisfaction flooding him even though he was still the one tied to the bed. "Agnoroth. Air dragon and fucking awesomely possessive lover."

Casey first stared at him as if he was nuts . . . then his eyes widened. "A-Air d-dragon?" His expression conveyed his disbelief.

Directly behind Casey, Agnoroth's form coalesced . . . as if his particles were being carried on the wind. While the dragon's speaking voice was a surprisingly high tenor, his growl was low, mean, and all dragon.

"Air dragon," Agnoroth whispered, anger flooding his tone. When he flicked his gaze to Kristof, his tone was immediately tempered, kind even. "Are you okay, my mate?"

"I'm okay . . . thanks to you."

Casey screamed, but it wasn't a fearful sound. Instead, it was full of rage. "No, damn you! If I can't have Kristof, no one can!" Spinning the shears in his hand, he returned his feral-eyed gaze to Kristof. He held the shears aloft as if they were a knife, obviously preparing to bring them down on him. "Die, motherfucker!"

Even as Casey raised the shears higher, Agnoroth was there in a flash . . . almost as if air bent around him, or he was air itself. He grabbed Casey's wrist with one hand while snagging his throat with the other. His hands weren't hands, but the iridescent-scaled claws that had caressed Kristof so carefully the day before.

They weren't so careful now.

The white talons sank deep into Casey's flesh. Blood sprayed across the covers, Kristof's flesh, and the walls. At the same time, Kristof stared into the vertically slitted eyes of his dragon.

Within seconds, Casey's throat had been yanked from him, and his body had been thrown across the room. Agnoroth picked up the shears and stalked after the fallen man. Spinning them in his grip, he struck, sinking the pointed ends deep into Casey's chest.

Agnoroth straightened and whirled. His dragon eyes swept over Kristof's form as he stalked closer. When he reached him, his sharp claws easily slashed through the ropes.

Then Agnoroth wrapped Kristof in his arms. "My mate,

my heart, my forever soul," he cried as tingles that could only be the dragon's magick danced across his skin.

"Yours," Kristof cried, clinging to his lover. "I knew you'd come."

"Always."

Then their forms seemed to swirl and blur and fly, and sensations that Kristof couldn't even begin to describe swept through him. He found himself outside the loft, clutched safely in Agnoroth's arms. As his lover soared them through the air, he reveled in how the wind whipped so perfectly through his hair and around his body.

Kristof clung, ecstasy thrumming through him. His dragon flew him to safety, their forms hidden by his magick, and he relished every wild second of it.

And I can't wait for the rest of my life's wild ride . . .

ABOUT THE CHARLIE RICHARDS

Charlie started writing fantasy when she was eight, and after stumbling onto her first erotic romance at age nineteen, she realized her true calling. She now focuses on writing gay erotic romance, normally of the paranormal variety, with heroes of all kinds. With the help and support of her husband, Charlie finally fulfilled one of her life-long goals . . . move to acreage with her horses. You can often find her curled up with her laptop and a cup of tea or glass of wine, creating her next adventure. Charlie enjoys exploring the mountains of her new Oregon home on horseback, 4-wheeler, or motorcycle.

She can be reached at ch.richards2010@yahoo.com
Or visit her at www.charlie-richards.com

Halloween Sabotage
Wyoming Shifters Short Stories
Book 2

By

Catherine Lievens

Who's sabotaging the Halloween party?

Griffith's plan was simple—organize a Halloween party for the kids who live in the shelter where he volunteers. Roark would have bowed out of it, but he couldn't let Armand organize it, not if they wanted all the kids to be in one piece by the end of the night, and the shelter not to be destroyed.

First, there's a flood, then a fire. North is sure someone is sabotaging the party, but who, and why? And will the council assassins be able to keep the party going, or will the kids be sorely disappointed?

CHAPTER ONE

R oark looked around the table, unable to stop smiling.
This was his family—his chosen family, the family that
wouldn't abandon him. His fellow assassins knew what this
life was like and what Roark had been through. They'd been
through it, too. *That* was why they were a real family.

They were noisy and messy, and a lot to deal with now that
Roark was partly in charge of them, but he wouldn't change
his life for anything in the world.

"I want to organize a Halloween party for the kids at the
shelter," Griffith declared.

Roark immediately changed his mind. He *did* want to
change his life. He could already see this was going to be a
mess, and he didn't want to be involved.

"What kind of party?" Armand asked, because of course
he was interested. Armand loved parties, any kind, for any
reason.

This *was* going to be a mess, wasn't it? And Roark would
be in charge of it, or at the very least, in charge of keeping an
eye on Armand and whoever else decided to participate.

"I don't know. They're teenagers, so probably no trick or
treating. Maybe something cute, like a dance party? They
don't really have the opportunity to have that."

Armand bounced on his chair. "It's a great idea, then. We
could rent a place big enough for them, decorate it, and prepare food. I've already picked my costume."

"No shifting into scary people," Roark warned.

Armand rolled his eyes. "I know better. They're kids. I

don't want to scare them." His eyes glinted with something that terrified Roark, though. "That means you're okay with it, then? We can do this?"

Roark wanted to say no. He didn't like parties, and he'd rather spend Halloween alone with his mate, in bed watching scary movies. Noel hated them, and he always ended up trying to climb into Roark's lap when they watched them because he was so afraid.

But Griffith was talking about kids — the kids who had to live in the LGBTQ shelter Griffith volunteered at because their families didn't want them, had kicked them out because of who they were. How was Roark supposed to say no to making them happy, at least for one evening? "On one condition."

Armand was bouncing so hard Roark half expected him to fall off his chair. It was cute and a good thing to see. Armand had been so hard on himself and closed off until Beck had walked into his life and pushed him to realize who he was — and that who he was was lovable. "What condition? We'll say yes to anything."

"I wouldn't promise that if I were you. I might ask you to take charge on the next mission that needs to be organized."

Armand grimaced. "You know I'm shit at organizing stuff."

"Then why do you want to organize a party? For kids who don't know us and who can never find out what we are and what we do, might I add."

"They don't need to know about the job. They don't need to know anything beyond the fact that we're Griffith's friends and that we want to help and make them happy for one night. Come on, Roark. Try to put yourself in their place. They don't have anything. They live in a shelter. They don't have a family or a home. This is the least we can do for them."

Roark put down his fork. "I know all that. You don't have to try to convince me. We'll do it. Well, everyone who wants to participate, anyway. And *I* will organize it." There was no way Roark was letting Armand have anything to do with the organization, or they'd end up partying in a ditch eating potato chips from the closest grocery store. That wouldn't do, not for Griffith's kids.

"I'm not protesting that part, trust me. You're more than welcome to think of everything. We'd probably end up without anything to drink if I had to do that."

"That's what I was thinking would happen."

Armand's smile was wide. "We're on, then?"

Roark looked at Griffith. "What do you think? Can you use our help? I promise Armand won't be in charge of anything."

That got a laugh out of Griffith. "I'll take all the help I can get, so yes, I agree."

"Good. I'm going to need your input. I don't organize parties that often, and never for kids."

"Well, they're not kids. They're teenagers."

"Does that make a difference?"

Griffith laughed. "Oh, you have so much to learn when it comes to teens, and probably kids, too."

"I should probably ask Payne to help, huh?"

"Probably."

Roark groaned. This was going to be more complicated than he'd hoped, wasn't it?

Hours later, he had his answer. Even though he wasn't in charge, Armand had insisted on helping, and Griffith had stuck around, too. They had a list of things to do, but it had been hard-won. Roark had had to shoot down several of Armand's ideas, including the one to rent a bouncy castle and the one to transform the shelter into a haunted house. Roark had been tempted by the last one, but the logistics to make it happen were too complicated, especially because Griffith had waited until the week before Halloween to come up with this.

They were going to have to make do with what they had, which Roark hoped would be enough. Several of the assassins had volunteered to help, and that would make things easier on him. That didn't change the fact that they didn't have a lot of time, though.

"It's going to be great," Armand said.

"Let's hope so."

"Oh, come on. Beck is going to take care of the music and the light stuff, Graham will cook, and you'll spend the evening glaring from a corner as you make sure everyone does what they have to do for the kids to have fun."

"I don't glare."

"Yeah, you do. And that's okay. It's one of the reasons we love you. You care so much about us, yet you don't want us to realize that you do. You're a huge teddy bear, really."

Roark growled, but instead of intimidating Armand, it only made him smile wider. "See? A big teddy bear. You'll make a great father one day."

That gave Roark pause. A father? Him?

That thought was as terrifying as the one to let Armand organize the party.

The only thing Noel wanted to do when he got home was getting a shower and flopping into bed. He wasn't supposed to come back this late, but one of his clients had been freaking out, and it had taken Noel a while to reassure him that he was doing everything he could to help him and that he shouldn't try to run and leave the country. That would only make things worse for him, and God knew the situation was already dire enough.

He punched in the code to the garage and drove his car inside, parking next to his mate's SUV. He waited until the garage door closed to turn off the car and lean back against the seat, closing his eyes for a moment. He had to go upstairs, but he needed a few minutes to gather the energy to do that.

He breathed in and out and relaxed. He was home. He'd eaten something on his way back, so he wouldn't have to stop in the kitchen for leftovers. He could go directly up to the room he shared with Roark, and if he was lucky, Roark would still be awake. They'd talk a bit before going to bed, and they'd cuddle and spend time together. Then he'd fall asleep in his mate's arms, and everything would be right in his world.

Everything was always right in Noel's world when he was with Roark, and even when he wasn't, because he knew that Roark was there to stay. They were bonded, linked for the rest of their lives. Roark would always be there for Noel to come home to.

Noel exited the car.

As he was stretching, his neck popped and cracked. He'd loosened his tie when he'd gotten into the car, and he took it off now, throwing it into his bag and closing the car. He wasn't surprised to see the light filtering from under the kitchen door when he climbed the stairs—there was always someone awake in the warehouse. There were so many of them—too many some days—coming and going, resting, eating, relaxing, and whatnot. Noel knew who was a night owl and who woke up early in the morning by now. The assassins and their mates were a lot to take in, messy and noisy on the best of days, but they were Roark's family, and now, Noel's.

Sometimes he wished he didn't have to deal with them, though, especially when he was tired.

He put in the code to the door and pushed it open, blinking at the light. He frowned when he saw that Roark was still there, sitting at the dining table along with Griffith, his mate Lawrence, Armand, and Beck. Roark was one of those who liked going to bed early so he could have some quiet time to read or watch TV. "Hey. I hope you weren't waiting for me. I texted you to tell you I'd be late," Noel said, dumping his bag onto the empty end of the table and walking to Roark. He kissed the back of Roark's neck and leaned on him, closing his eyes and inhaling his mate's scent.

He would have been too self-conscious to do something like that a few years ago, but the warehouse was his home, the assassins his family, and that came with some perks, one of which was that Noel was entirely comfortable with them.

Roark reached back and squeezed Noel's arm. "I wasn't planning on waiting for you here, but Griffith had an idea, and I had to stay if I didn't want Armand to make a mess."

"An idea?"

"I want to throw a Halloween party for the shelter kids," Griffith said.

It took Noel a second to understand what he was talking about. Griffith had only recently moved in, and Noel didn't know him that well yet. He *did* know that Griffith volunteered at an LGBTQ shelter, though. The shelter worked with teenagers who needed help, providing them with food, medical attention, or a bed—and sometimes all three of those. Noel had meant to ask if he could help, maybe volunteer, too, but he'd been too busy and hadn't had the time to approach Griffith about it yet. "That sounds like a good idea."

Griffith smiled. "I want to give them something they can remember, something they don't usually have. Armand volunteered to plan it, but Roark took over."

Noel chuckled and kissed Roark's neck before straightening up. "Trust me, Roark saved your ass."

Griffith chuckled. "I wasn't aware of that, but I've just heard enough stories to realize now."

Noel bumped Roark's shoulder. "You're going to organize a party, then?"

Roark groaned and leaned the back of his head against

Noel's stomach. "I know. What was I thinking?"

"That the party would be a mess if you let Armand do it."

"Hey!" Armand protested, but they all knew he *would* have made a mess.

Noel smiled and kissed the tip of Roark's nose. "I'm going to bed. Are you staying down here to continue planning this party of yours?"

"I think we did enough planning for the day. Armand, you're not allowed to organize anything without me, Win, or Griffith present. Got it?"

Armand pouted. "Whatever. I'm not *that* bad at stuff."

Noel kissed Armand on the cheek. "You're a good man, but you're hopeless at organizing anything."

Noel was glad when he and Roark finally got to their room. The silence there was soothing after the day he'd had, and he couldn't wait to get into bed with his mate and rest. He made a beeline for the bathroom, knowing Roark had showered before dinner. This was their routine, and there was something soothing about it, something that made Noel feel like he was home.

Roark was in bed when Noel came out of the shower, steam billowing behind him. He was reading, but he put down his book and smiled. He looked tired, and Noel knew he was still struggling with being one of those who gave the orders now. He was doing his best to help Win, but it wasn't always easy, especially with so many people to deal with, now that a lot of the assassins had found their mates.

Noel slid under the sheets naked, sighing in pleasure and closing his eyes at the feeling of the cool, clean sheets against his still-damp skin. He started to relax, but before he could, Roark rolled him to his front. Noel yelped, but he let his mate guide him. Roark climbed on top of him, straddling his ass, and pushed his fingers into the knots in Noel's shoulder.

Noel groaned in pleasure. "A bit more to the right," he

said, wiggling his right shoulder.

Roark chuckled and leaned down to place a kiss there. "Always so demanding."

"You're the one who decided to give me a massage. You didn't even ask if I wanted one."

Roark's hands stopped moving. "Do you want me to stop, then?"

Noel turned his head to glare at his mate. "Don't you dare."

Roark laughed and started moving his fingers again. "That's what I thought. Don't fall asleep on me, though."

"Why? Did you have more plans for me? I'm kind of tired."

"Too tired for me?"

"I suppose it depends on what you have in mind."

As an answer, Roark tilted his hips forward. He was naked, like Noel, and he was hard. His cock glided against the skin of Noel's lower back and his buttocks, and Noel sighed in pleasure. "Maybe not too tired."

Roark leaned forward until his lips brushed against Noel's ear. "You don't have to do anything. Just stay there. Don't move. I'll take care of you."

He always did, and this time wasn't any different.

Roark moved away, but Noel stayed where he was. He listened to the sounds his mate made with a smile on his face. He recognized the opening and closing of the nightstand drawer, and he knew exactly what Roark was planning. He'd learned his mate since they'd first met.

When Roark touched Noel again, his fingers were slick with lube. He didn't pry Noel's ass cheeks apart but instead coated the inside of his thighs, then climbed on top of him again. Noel pressed his legs together and raised his hips, and Roark slid a hand under his body, wrapping his fingers around Noel's cock. That and the pressure of Roark's cock between his thighs, stroking and pushing against his balls and his taint every time Roark thrust back and forth, was more than enough to bring Noel to completion.

They didn't need to fuck every night. This was just as good, just as close and intimate as penetration.

And it was easier to clean up, something for which Noel was glad, since he'd just showered.

CHAPTER TWO

Armand knew he was bouncing rather than walking, and he didn't even care. Today was Halloween, and he *loved* Halloween.

It wasn't only because he got to shift into whoever and whatever he wanted, at least not this year. No, this year, he was thinking bigger. When Griffith had volunteered him to help organize a party for his shelter kids, he'd jumped on the opportunity. He missed the kids he'd saved from that warehouse, even though two of them still lived with him and the others at the warehouse. He wanted to do more good stuff, to help more, and while he supposed some people would say he did more than enough through his job, some days, it didn't feel like it.

Armand didn't mind being an assassin. He didn't mind killing people, not when those people more than deserved it. Hell, he'd have gladly killed some of them twice if he could have. But he couldn't, and while ridding the world of them was a good thing, he wanted to do *more*.

Armand had been lucky to find a new family when he left the lab, but the kids at the shelter hadn't had that luck. They'd lived on the streets because of something they couldn't change, which was a bit like the parents kicking their kids out because they were shifters. It wasn't something that was chosen, and it wasn't something anyone could change. They all needed support, and Armand was more than happy to volunteer, even if it was only for a party.

The fact that it was Halloween and that he got to help

decorate the place Roark had rented was a bonus.

Armand walked toward the office to get the keys to the banquet space. It wasn't big, nowhere near the biggest one in the building, but then, it didn't need to be, since there weren't that many kids at the shelter. They probably could have organized everything there, but Griffith had thought it would be nice for the kids to leave the shelter for one evening, under plenty of supervision. They spent most of their time there, between studying and looking for work.

Besides, Graham had demanded a decent kitchen space when he'd agreed to take care of the food for the party, and from what Griffith had said, the kitchen at the shelter was barely enough to cook for the group of kids staying there.

Armand pushed open the door and grinned at the man behind the counter. "Hello! I'm here about one of the banquet spaces you rent, the smaller one. We reserved it for the day."

The man frowned. "You didn't get my message?"

That didn't sound good. "What message?"

"The one where I told you that there was a problem and that you couldn't use the space anymore."

"A problem? What kind of problem?" Armand could probably face small things, but from the look on the man's face, it wasn't a little thing they were talking about.

"Flooding. A pipe broke during the night, and we found out this morning when we came in. The entire space you rented is flooded, and the others are already booked. I'm sorry, but there's no way you can organize your party here."

"Are you sure? I can call someone to help with the pipes, and we can clean up." They needed this space. It was the only one they'd managed to find since they decided so late to do this party. Not having it might mean having to cancel the party, and Armand wasn't going to allow that to happen.

"I'm sorry," the man repeated. He grimaced. "We already have a plumber working on it, but it's going to take at least a few days to pump the water out and dry the space entirely. I'm sorry about this, and I wish I could do more. I'll give you your deposit back, of course."

Armand shook his head. "It's fine. Keep the deposit." He'd probably need it to pay the plumber because those things could get expensive. It wasn't like Armand couldn't afford it anyway. "I'm sorry that happened, and I hope you won't lose too much money or business. Thank you."

Armand was not bouncing anymore when he left the office. What was he supposed to do now? What were *they* supposed to do? They'd already told the kids about the party, and that meant it had to happen. No one wanted to disappoint the kids. They'd already gone through enough of that in their short lives.

Armand took his phone out and dialed Griffith's number. He should call Roark, but the man was with his mate, and Armand wasn't going to interrupt *that*.

"Armand?"

Armand sighed in relief. At least Griffith had answered. "We can't use the banquet space we rented."

"What? Why not?"

"It flooded. The owner was talking about cleaning up, but it's going to take a few days, and Halloween is today."

"You don't have to remind me of that. I know Halloween is today. Dammit. The kids were so excited. They haven't been able to talk about anything else in the past few days."

"What do we do now?"

"We'll have to use the shelter. The living room is tiny compared to the banquet room, of course, but it will have to make do. It's not like they're not used to fitting in there altogether, and as long as we keep an eye on them, everything should be fine."

"All right. I'll go there right away. I have the decorations and everything else in my car."

Griffith sighed. "I'll let everyone involved know about this. We'll meet you there. Hopefully, the space is big enough that Beck can decorate it. It's going to be hard to keep the kids away from the living room while he does it, though."

Armand grinned. "Leave that to me."

Griffith chuckled. "I should have known you'd volunteer for this. You're just as much a kid as they are."

"Hell, yes, I am."

"Be careful with them, though, Armand. I know you're excited about this, and that you mean well, but some of these kids have been through hell and back, and they're going to be wary of you."

"I know, and I'll be careful." Armand might be playful, but he'd been through his own hell. He wasn't going to push anyone, and he certainly wasn't going to scare the kids. He *would* make sure they had fun, though, every single one of them.

"This isn't going to work," Beck said, his hands on his hips as he perused the room in front of him.

Griffith bumped into him as he passed by him, his arms full of bags. "You're going to *have* to make it work because we don't have an alternative."

"What about that banquet space you rented?" They'd sent him pictures, and Beck had told them it would be okay to set up everything. If they wanted him to organize visual effects and whatnot, he needed enough space to do it, and the living room in front of him didn't have that space.

Griffith sighed and put down the bags. "Flooded, and there's no way we can find anything else even remotely similar over the next few hours. Graham is working in the kitchen and doing what he can with the stuff that's there. You're going to have to do the same. I know it won't be anything like what you planned, but this is better than nothing."

Beck huffed. "All right, all right. I'll work with this, and I'll see what I can do." Which wouldn't be much since the living room was smaller than the one they had at home. Beck had planned a lot of lights and sounds, as well as spooky effects, but he wasn't even sure where he could hide the projectors here. He couldn't. He was going to have to redo all his plans, dammit.

"I know this isn't ideal," Griffith added. "I'm sorry. I'm sure we can find someone else if you want to pass, or maybe skip the music and whatnot entirely."

Beck resisted the urge to slap Griffith upside the head, only because he didn't know the man that well yet. Griffith and Lawrence had only gotten together recently, and while he was a good man—working at the shelter was a sign of that—Beck had no idea how he'd react. "Don't be stupid. Of course I'll do it. As long as you're aware of the fact that it's not going to be as good as what I had planned." Beck had never backed down from a challenge, and this was exactly that.

Griffith smiled. "I know, and I know it's not your fault. It's no one's fault. But it's okay, Beck. These kids aren't used to parties and this kind of fun. The shelter is always hard-pressed for money, even with the donations."

Beck didn't point out that if Griffith wanted, he could prob-ably get his grandfather to donate enough to keep the shelter wealthy for several years. It wasn't Griffith's money, not yet, and he was doing what he could to help. It was already much more than a lot of people did, and it made Beck feel like he didn't do enough.

He cleared his throat. "Well, this is going to be the best party any of them has ever been to."

Griffith's smile was gentle. "Good. They deserve it."

Beck got to work. He could hear other people working around the house, in the kitchen, and the hallway, and he

knew they were all doing everything they could for the kids —
teenagers, really. But whatever happened, they'd have a great
Halloween, and that was the important part of this.

"What did you have in mind in here?" Armand said as he
wandered in. He was eating a cupcake that he'd no doubt stolen from Graham. The cupcake itself was green, while the
frosting was orange and black with small sugar spiders on it.
Or at least Beck hoped they were made of sugar.

"We're going to keep the room dark, of course, and set up
a few mannequins in the corners. I have too many, so we'll
have to choose. What do you think? Vampire? Mummy?
Zombie?"

Armand wrinkled his nose. "Maybe not the zombie? I
mean, I don't know how true to life it is, but we're going to
have stuff to eat, and they're not exactly appetizing." He
leaned toward Beck to kiss him, but Beck slapped a hand over
his mouth. "I don't think so."

"Why not?"

"That cupcake has spiders on it."

Armand rolled his eyes. "Not real ones."

"Are you sure about that?"

Armand raised the cupcake and looked at it closer. Beck
was pretty sure the spiders *were* fake, but he still grimaced
when Armand shrugged and gave the cupcake another bite.

"Whatever they are, they're tasty."

"That's because Graham baked them, and he's going to
kick your ass if he discovers you're stealing them. They're for
the kids."

Armand's face started shifting, and Beck knew what he
was going to do before he did it. He slapped the back of his
mate's head and glared at him. "No shifting into a teenager,
Armand."

Armand pouted. "Why not? I'm hungry."

"Because I wouldn't be able to have sex with you again if I

ever saw a teenage you run around."

Armand gaped. "That's a good reason."

"I know it is."

"No shifting, then. But I want a kiss."

"Not if you keep eating that creepy stuff."

"It's sugar, honey."

Beck had to laugh, and yes, he had to kiss his mate. Armand could be ridiculous sometimes, but he cared, and that was what mattered.

A loud beeping interrupted them—which was probably good, since they could get carried away sometimes—and Armand jerked away and dropped his cupcake. He looked forlorn, but before he could whine about it, Beck noticed smoke coming from the hallway.

"Something's wrong," he said, pushing Armand away and rushing toward the kitchen, because *of course* that was where the smoke was coming from.

He couldn't see anything when he stepped into the room. Thick smoke filled the space, and several people were coughing and swearing.

"Open the damn window!" Graham yelled.

"That's what I was trying to do!" Griffith yelled back. "I can't *find* the window!"

Beck put a hand on the wall and used it to guide himself to the window. He wasn't sure how much good that would do, but it wasn't like they could do anything else right now.

He felt like he was about to cough his lungs out by the time he was back in the hallway. Armand looked like he wanted to strangle him, no doubt because he'd scared him, but Beck turned his attention to Graham and Griffith. "What happened?" he asked.

Graham's face was red. "I don't know. The cookies shouldn't have burned. I hadn't put them in the oven long enough for them to. It has to be the oven." He raked a hand through his hair. "How am I supposed to get all the food ready without the oven?"

Armand whimpered. "It's cursed."

Beck had no idea what he was talking about. "What do you mean?"

"The party. It's cursed. First, there was the flooding, now this."

Beck groaned. What Armand was saying was bullshit, but he couldn't deny it *did* feel like the party was cursed.

CHAPTER THREE

Milo couldn't look away from the disaster that was now the shelter's kitchen. He had no idea what went wrong, and replacing the oven wouldn't be a problem, but what about the party? And those poor cookies looked like they'd been baked directly in Satan's oven.

"What now?" he asked Graham. Everyone else had smartly disappeared from the kitchen—Armand had left with two more cupcakes—but Milo knew they'd come back if they were needed, and they might be. He and Graham needed to decide what needed to be done first.

Graham rubbed his face, leaving traces of flour on his cheek. "I don't know. We obviously can't use the oven, so anything that still needs to be baked is out, and we still had a lot of that to do."

Milo's eyes burned, and it wasn't because of the smoke still coming out of the oven. He'd volunteered to help because he wanted the kids who lived at the shelter to have a fun evening, to be able to forget all their problems for a few hours. They could still do that, but Graham had put a lot of work in the food, and half of it had gone down in flames. "What happened to the oven, anyway?" he asked, moving closer and leaning to see inside.

A hand grabbed his arm and pulled him back. "What do you think you're doing?" his mate asked. North was angry, but Milo knew it wasn't at him.

"I was just looking."

"That smoke is bad for you. What happened? I leave for

half an hour, and you two try to burn down the kitchen?"

"We didn't do anything!" Milo protested. "I don't know what happened. The oven worked just fine until now."

North looked at the cookies and cupcakes Milo and Graham had already baked, some already decorated. "That's weird. Did the two of you leave the kitchen together?"

"We had to go grab some stuff from the car."

"How long were you gone?"

Milo cocked his head. "Ten minutes, maybe? One of the bags broke, and we had to gather all the stuff that fell. What are you saying, North?"

North shook his head. "Nothing. What can I do to help?"

"Unless you have a tiny oven in your pocket . . ."

"I don't, but I *do* have a phone, and I can call Dasha and ask him to shimmer the two of you back home so you can use the kitchen there. I don't know why you didn't do that right away."

"Because I didn't want to have to be shimmered back and forth," Graham snapped. "This was easier, and we could continue to put food together even once the party started."

Milo leaned against North. He needed comfort, even if it made him a wimp. He just wanted a moment to let the bad feelings wash over him. Then he'd be able to push them away and focus on a solution.

North wrapped his arm around Milo's shoulders and kissed his forehead. "We'll find a solution," he murmured, and Milo believed him. They were stronger together, and now that Milo felt even slightly better, he could think instead of crying.

He straightened. "Okay, let's do this. Graham, start packing the things we're going to need. North, call Dasha. I know he was planning to help anyway today, so he probably won't mind. If we need more shimmering, we can ask the twins. It's about time they leave the infirmary."

"What are you planning?" North asked.

"We can finish the baking back home. We'll need someone to shimmer back and forth with the stuff once it's ready, but we can do the decorating here, and if once the party starts, if there's not enough food, we can always grab some pizza. Most kids love pizza, and the ones who don't can stick to the stuff we've gotten ready."

Graham finally smiled. "That sounds like a plan."

"It's the best we can do with the little time we have. We're going to have to make do." Milo wasn't looking forward to the cleaning up that would be involved here, or having to talk to the people who ran the shelter. He and Graham would make sure the shelter got a new oven, possibly an even better one, but that would take some time, and he wasn't looking forward to admitting how much of a mess they'd made, even though he had no idea what had happened.

"Do you need anything from the store? I can grab Armand or someone else and go," North suggested.

Milo's heart felt like it was swelling in his chest. He knew it was something trivial, but North offering himself to help made him feel loved, even though this wasn't about him.

He wrapped his arms around North's waist and kissed his cheek. "Thank you."

North's cheeks flushed a light pink. "We're in this together, yeah? We decided we were going to do whatever we had to make sure these kids have fun tonight, so we are. You and Graham focus on the baking and whatever else you were planning to do. You can use me as your errand boy."

Graham cleared his throat. "We should have everything we need, but thank you."

North nodded and took out his phone. "Good. Let me call Dasha, and we'll organize the transport back and forth."

They were in this together, all of them, and they were going to make it work.

North waited until Milo was safely out of sight to glare at the oven. He had no idea what had happened, but he didn't believe in coincidences, and between the flooding and the fire, he was sure something was happening. He knew most people wouldn't believe him on that, so he went to the one person who would—Roark. He needed to know about the fire anyway, so he could start organizing for a new oven to be purchased and brought here.

He found Roark outside, in the shelter's tiny backyard. He was talking with Griffith and one of the people who took care of the kids while they all kept an eye on them. North counted seven teenagers, and he stayed as far away from them as he could, because he wasn't good with teenagers, or with kids, or with people in general, to be honest. "Roark?"

Roark leaned closer to Griffith to tell him something, then rose from the bench and came to North. "What happened inside? We kept the kids out here to be safe, but we heard shouting coming from the kitchen. Has Graham tried to kill Armand because he was stealing too much food?"

The kitchen window opened on the street rather than on the yard, so Roark had no idea they'd just avoided a fire. "You should see this."

Roark arched a brow, but he followed North inside. "That sounds more serious than I thought."

"As it is, it's going to cost us a new oven, but that's the only thing that was ruined, along with the batch of cookies that was inside."

Roark grimaced. "That's why Graham was yelling."

"Yes. But don't you think it's a bit too much of a coincidence?"

"What do you mean?" Roark peered inside the oven.

North knew what he'd seen—a tray with the charcoal

remains of the cookies, walls black with soot, and some smoke still coming out. The window was wide open, but the room smelled of burned things.

"First, there was the flooding."

Roark straightened. "That was a burst pipe."

"That we know of, but I doubt Armand hung around to make sure that's what happened. Then there's the oven that worked perfectly until now and suddenly didn't."

"Graham did manage to bake a few batches of cupcakes, though."

"He would have, if the person who tampered with the oven made sure to do something that would take a little time to work out."

Roark leaned back against the counter and crossed his arms over his chest. "How does someone even tamper with an oven? I'm not saying you're wrong, but I don't know if that's possible."

"Maybe not, but do you remember the last time coincidences added up?"

Roark grimaced. "That weekend was a shit show. At least we managed to have fun once we caught that guy."

"Yeah, but we never heard about him again."

"You think he's still after me? I'm not sure it makes sense."

"Some people can hold a grudge, and there's the fact that you humiliated him *again*. I wouldn't be surprised if he tried to get to you a second time."

"He hasn't until now, and it's been almost a year."

"True. That doesn't mean he's not around here somewhere lurking and waiting for his chance to strike. And if he *is* here, the situation is dangerous for the kids. The party would be the perfect occasion for this guy to get his revenge, and I don't know if he'd stop in front of the kids."

Roark nodded. "If he or anyone else is here, we need to find them."

"That's' what I was thinking." *This* was something North was good at. Not at talking with people, not at taking care of any of them but Milo, but this. He supposed it *was* a way of taking care of them, though. He could use his training to find the threat and get rid of it.

They separated and combed through the shelter room by room. They had to tell the woman in charge about it as to not frighten the teenagers who lived there. North hadn't spoken to any of them, but he could too easily imagine what some of them had gone through, and he didn't want to freak them out.

North found him in a broom closet upstairs.

He almost laughed in his face when he opened the door and found Julian with his back pressed against the wall, his front so close to the vacuum cleaner that he could have kissed it just by puckering his lips.

Julian glared at North as North crossed his arms over his chest and leaned his shoulder against the frame of the door. "I'd ask why you're here, but I suspect I already know," North drawled.

"Where is Roark?"

North rolled his eyes. "Around. How's that vacuum cleaner treating you? You look cozy."

"I'm going to find Roark, and I'm going to—"

"Make out with the vacuum cleaner, yeah, I got that. And why the fuck would you think that coming here of all places to get back at Roark for whatever imaginary slight he did to you was a good idea?"

"I wanted to ruin his party. I thought he'd cancel it when I flooded the place he'd rented, and when he didn't, I followed him here."

"And you tampered with the oven without noticing that this is an LGBTQ shelter for teenagers."

Julian's eyes widened. "What?"

"Are you sure you're a professional killer? Because not

researching this place doesn't sound professional to me."

"I didn't have the time to research!"

"Whatever. So you decided it would be a good idea to ruin the Halloween party Roark organized for those poor kids who've been kicked out of their houses and had to go through hell and back just because you have a grudge. Got it."

Julian wiggled out of the closet. North stepped back to let him pass. He doubted Julian would have tried to kill Roark this time around—not that he had the first time. It sounded more like he was trying to ruin his day than like he wanted to hurt him, and so far, he'd very much managed to do that.

"I want to make it up to the kids," Julian said.

"Good. You can leave. That should do it."

"I want to do more. It's my fault that this party is ruined."

"Who said it was? Graham and Milo went back home to bake there, so that's not going to be a problem." But North did *not* want to clean up the kitchen, and since Julian had offered to help . . ."But I do have something for you to do. That is, if Roark doesn't try to rip your head off first, of course. I doubt he's going to be happy to find you here and to realize you're the one creating all these problems and sabotaging our party."

Julian paled just a bit, but he nodded. "You can tell him."

"I will, and not because I have your authorization."

"But I do want to help, so it would probably be better for you to wait."

"Maybe, but Roark isn't an idiot. He's going to know what happened once he sees you. I don't think he's going to try to kill you here, though, if that makes you feel better. He won't want the kids to be traumatized. But I'd run as soon as possible if I were you, although it would be fun to watch Roark kick your ass." But Milo cared about the party, and that meant that North cared about it, too, more so than he cared about watching Julian getting his ass kicked.

Epilogue

The party was a success, and Griffith was relieved. For a moment—okay, maybe more than a moment considering what had happened—he'd thought he'd have to pull the plug on it and just buy a few pizzas for the kids. But now there was spooky music, the living room was dark and filled with people, food, and even a few life-sized mummies and vampires that kind of freaked Griffith out.

The kids were having fun. Griffith had heard more than one squeak of pleasure when they'd first walked into the living room, and now they were talking and dancing and eating their own weight in food. The shelter would have a new oven as soon as it could be delivered, and it had already been paid for by an anonymous good Samaritan that was probably the guy who'd almost made it explode.

Several assassins were there. They were all careful around the kids, and after what had happened with that Julian guy, they were present more to keep an eye on things than to have fun, but they'd dressed up to make the kids more comfortable. It worked—although in Armand's case, the *assassins* were the ones uncomfortable now, since he'd shifted into Win and had decided to dress up as a Disney princess. He'd already knocked down a small table with his big blue gown, his tiara was crooked, and he was trying to give the assassins orders while they attempted to avoid him. Griffith had to admit the sight was weird, and he knew Win wouldn't be happy about this. It *was* funny, though.

Griffith wasn't sure if Noel and Armand had coordinated

their costumes on purpose, but Noel was dressed as a prince, with a fake plastic sword and shining blond hair. Roark hadn't dressed up, and while North hadn't *wanted* to dress up, Milo had convinced him to stick a pair of fake fangs in his mouth, and he kept snarling at Milo—who made a scrawny Jon Snow under the huge fake fur coat he wore—to show them off. Beck was in the corner to keep the lights, sounds, and music under control, and Griffith couldn't help but wonder how comfortable he was sitting in his full Iron Man costume.

Griffith leaned closer to Lawrence so his mate could hear him. "What was that guy's problem anyway? Julian." Knowing that a grown adult had managed to find his way into the shelter left Griffith feeling cold and wary, even though he knew that most people wouldn't be able to get through the door. This guy was a professional assassin, from what he knew, and while that should no doubt have scared him even more than he already was, he knew enough assassins to be aware of the fact that not all of them were bad guys. This one hadn't been, even though he'd made a mess of things and had nearly killed the party.

Lawrence shrugged. "Not sure. I know he tried to get to Roark when he and some of the others went for a weekend in the mountains last year. They had to kick his ass then, but they let him go. I guess he's at it again."

Griffith looked around. "Are you guys sure it was okay to let him go again?"

Lawrence patted his arm. "Don't worry. I'm sure North and Roark kept an eye on him until he was out of sight, and even though he did what he did, he also helped with the clean-up."

"And he paid for a new oven."

Lawrence grinned. "Yeah?"

"I think it was him, anyway. I doubt Roark found the time

to order a new one yet, but I got an email with the info earlier. It's going to be delivered tomorrow."

"Doesn't sound like a bad guy to me."

"Well, he *did* try to get to Roark." Although to be honest, Griffith still wasn't sure what the party had to do with it. The guy didn't seem to have wanted to kill Roark, just to annoy him by ruining a party he thought was for him.

"If this guy is like us, he could have gotten to Roark easily enough. He had more than one opportunity to hurt the people here, yet he didn't. I think he just wanted to prank Roark or something like that, and he didn't realize that the party wasn't for him."

Griffith leaned against Lawrence, who wrapped an arm around him. "Life with you guys is never boring, that's for sure." He kissed Lawrence's cheek, doing his best to avoid ruining the snake make-up he'd decided would do as a Halloween costume.

"You should have suspected that when you learned who we are and what we do."

"I wouldn't change my life for anything in the world." Griffith needed Lawrence to know that. He knew that his mate still wondered sometimes, because of what had been done to him, because of the venom in his system, but they'd found a way around it, and life was good.

"Hi."

Griffith smiled at Tay, who was hovering in front of him and Lawrence. He was wearing a dress, his hair was up, and his eyes were beautifully made up with eyeliner and glitter. His smile was tentative, though, and Griffith hated that. He wanted Tay—and all the other kids—to feel comfortable, especially at the shelter. "What's up? Are you enjoying yourself?"

Tay's gaze moved from Griffith to Lawrence, then back to Griffith. "I didn't know you had a boyfriend."

"Well, Lawrence isn't my boyfriend. He's my mate."

Tay's eyes widened. "So he's a shifter?"

"Yes, and he's right there. You can talk to him, you know."

Tay's eyes narrowed, and he turned to Lawrence. "I'm a boy."

"Me, too," Lawrence said, not missing a beat.

"I'm not dressed like this because of the party. Well, yes, I am, but not because it's a Halloween party. I wanted to look pretty."

"And you do, very much so."

Tay blinked. He'd probably expected Lawrence to tell him boys shouldn't dress the way he was, and he was obviously surprised that wasn't the answer he'd gotten. "Thank you?" he squeaked, making it sound like a question.

Lawrence's smile softened. "You're welcome. And you *do* look pretty. Are you enjoying yourself?"

Tay looked around the room. "Yes. I—we didn't expect this. I mean, we knew about the party, obviously, but we thought it was going to be a few pizzas and a scary movie or something."

"That's why we did it. You guys deserve to have fun. I know everyone here does what they can, including me, but we thought you could use a break, some fun before going back to your everyday life. You *are* having fun, right?"

"Of course we are! The decorations are awesome, and you guys have the best costumes. And the food. It's so good. I can't stop eating it. Thank you for everything."

Griffith wanted to hug Tay, but he knew better than to try touching any of the kids. "You're welcome. Now, why don't you go have fun? Just, leave me a few of those cupcakes, yeah?" Graham would be happy to know his food was being enjoyed just as much as it usually was. He'd worked hard today, and he still was, hidden away in the kitchen, where he was making sure the food was brought out in waves rather

67

than all dumped at once on the tables they'd managed to fit in the living room after pushing the furniture against the walls.

The grin on Tay's face hurt to see, but in a good way. Tay, like all the other kids in the shelter, deserved to be smiling like that every day for the rest of their lives. Griffith and the others did what they could, but the best solution would be to find families for the kids, people who would give them a home and the love they needed. Griffith couldn't help with that, but he could help with making them as happy as possible in this situation, and now that he'd found Lawrence and his family, he knew he wouldn't be the only one. Those who'd helped with the party had been touched by the kids' stories, and Griffith knew the shelter had just earned a bunch of volunteers, and probably a whole lot of money.

The Halloween party had served more than one purpose, even with the guy trying to sabotage it.

About the Catherine Lievens

Catherine lives in Italy, country of good food and hot men. She used to write fantasy as a child, but it was reading her first gay erotic romance novel that made her realize that that was what she really wanted to write.

After graduating from college in English language and translation, she divides her day between writing, reading, taking care of her son and reading some more.

You can find her on Facebook and Twitter or on her website: authorcatherinelievens.wordpress.com

Email: lievens.catherine@gmail.com

Newsletter: http://eepurl.com/c-uvKn

Harvest Blessings

By

Liza Kay

In Paw's Cove, every season has a reason for joy . . .

When Kirill mated with Alpha Andrei Bazin, little did he realize his organizational skills would be put to the test! While Andrei is occupied with training his enforcers, speaking with prospective clan members, and overseeing construction of new houses for the growing clan, Kirill finds himself at the helm of the Paw's Cove Harvest Festival and Feast. Daunted barely describes how Kirill is feeling—overwhelmed and inadequate may be closer to the mark.

Kirill's gung-ho assistant is wearing him down with her enthusiasm for the upcoming event, and she's also bringing out his insecurities about his place in the pack. Add to that the impending birth of Kirill and Andrei's first child, carried by Andrei's cousin Mary, who graciously offered to be their surrogate, and Kirill has a whole lot on his mind and on his plate.

Kirill and Andrei are finding it difficult to have alone time what with all the various demands being placed on them. But they have to hold it together, for the sake of the clan and for their unborn child. More than an annual festival, this harvest blessing will bring a joy like no other.

DEDICATION

For my readers.

CHAPTER ONE

"And these are the proposals for the stage decorations. I pre-selected three designs you can choose from. Personally, I think we should go with the same color scheme we picked for the wagons and the marching band uniforms." Haley leaned over his shoulder and placed another stack of folders on the desk. Her strawberry scent was extremely strong today. Kirill couldn't help but sneeze.

He grabbed a tissue from the box on his desk and blew his nose. "Haley, why are you doing this to me?"

She sighed, threw back her long hair in one of her typical grand gestures, and placed her hands on her hips. "Well, *you* wanted the job."

"I don't remember volunteering to be the chooser of color schemes and marching band uniforms." He slammed his pen on the desk in frustration and leaned back in his chair. Reaching up, he tried to massage the knots out of his neck. Kirill sure as fuck had more important things to worry about this time of the year than décor or fashion choices.

"You volunteered to become alpha mate, genius. Congratulations. You didn't think the position only involved hot sex with the alpha, did you?" Haley squeezed his shoulder with a huge grin and an inappropriate wink.

"And there goes that hope." Kirill rubbed his eyes. "Why don't *you* pick the stage decorations? You're more passionate when it comes to the festival than I am."

"Paw's Cove is *your* home, Kirill. And the annual Harvest Festival and Feast is one of the most important events in town!

We've been celebrating this day since the town was founded—"

"By the first alpha in 1895. *I know.*"

Haley sniffed and lifted her nose. "Right. He was a great-great-great-whatever grandfather of mine. So show some respect and decide on the fucking decorations, will you? There's only three weeks left until the big day."

When the door opened, Kirill sighed in relief. Only one man had the balls to enter his office without knocking. "Thank God! Rescue me."

Andrei sauntered into the room, a smirk on his sexy face and a twinkle in his ice blue eyes. "Haley." He dipped his head. "Busy driving my mate crazy again? Have some mercy. He's a father-to-be."

"His stress level will only increase once the munchkin is born." Haley left her spot behind Kirill and walked toward Andrei. "If he can't organize one tiny festival without breaking down, how will he—"

Andrei lifted his hand. "Enough. You earned yourself a break, Haley. Leave us alone."

Haley immediately lowered her gaze and offered her neck to Andrei as she hurried past him. She closed the door quietly behind her, leaving them together.

"I wish I had your talent for shutting her up." Kirill threw his hands in the air and growled. "What the hell do I know about color schemes?" He gave the pile on his desk a shove. "It's a fucking harvest festival with a huge potluck for the whole village. Why does it *need* a color scheme?" When Andrei laughed, Kirill shot up from his chair and pointed at his mate. "Don't you dare laugh at me. I'm stuck in this damn office all day while Haley tortures me with flower arrangements and pumpkin pie recipes while you spend your days wrestling with your enforcers."

"I prefer the word *training*." Andrei raised a brow. He

leaned lazily against the edge of Kirill's desk and crossed his arms over his wide chest. The thin brown shirt he wore stretched almost obscenely over his drool-worthy muscles. And the bulge hidden behind the fly of his worn jeans . . . *yum.*

Kirill licked his lips. "Come to think of it, why are you so clean? And you smell of sandalwood. Usually, after you've been training, you visit me all dirty, smelly, and bloody." Kirill didn't mind. Rugged Andrei, fresh from training, never failed to turn him on.

Andrei leaned down and reached for the handle on the bottom drawer of Kirill's desk. He grinned as he slowly slid it open. "Today's a special day. Check your calendar."

Kirill huffed as he watched Andrei root around the drawer. "What? Did you make a *sex on desk with my mate* entry?"

"Nah." Andrei pulled out a bottle of lube, shook it, and eyed the clear liquid critically. "Although I considered it, since we haven't had much one-on-one time lately. Does lube have an expiration date?" He frowned.

Growling, Kirill snatched the bottle from Andrei's grip and stood. "Over the past few months, twelve new businesses have opened in town. At least once a week bears who want to move to Paw's Cove request to join the clan. And five new houses are under construction on clan lands even as we speak. Some members of the clan have had trouble accepting me, so I've had to work extra hard to convince them we're a good team." Kirill opened the bottle and sniffed the content. "Of *course* we haven't had much us time. And Mary—"

Andrei cupped his face and tilted it up. "I know it hasn't been easy, honey muffin."

Closing his eyes, Kirill snuggled against his mate. "But so worth it. Loving you, falling asleep and waking up beside you, is worth all the trouble."

"I love you, too." Andrei kissed him, softly at first but with rising urgency. "*Need* you," he said against Kirill's mouth. He nipped Kirill's lip as he pushed between him and the desk.

"Take me. I'm yours." Kirill flexed his hips, teasing his hardness against the bulge in Andrei's pants.

"Nope." Andrei waggled his eyebrows. "You need some stress release." He hooked his fingers under the waistband of Kirill's jeans and quickly unsnapped the button fly. "And that's exactly what I'll give you." Andrei lowered to his knees and quickly peeled down Kirill's jeans. "Damn, those are tight." He laughed when he finally freed Kirill and his prick bobbed freely.

Kirill ran his fingers through Andrei's messy black hair and tugged at the strands. "Sucking now, fashion tips later."

Andrei looked up at him and slowly licked the head of Kirill's cock. "Sucking's not all you want, right?" He blew over the wet tip, closed his lips around it, and suckled.

Kirill shuddered and tightened his hold on Andrei's hair. "Shit." He thrust forward into the hot, wet cavern of his mate's mouth. He growled when Andrei choked. "Not so smug now, are you?"

Andrei moaned and grabbed Kirill's ass cheeks. He took a deep breath, then sucked Kirill to the base until his nose touched the smooth skin of his groin. When he came up for air he coughed. "Damn, I love it when you're rough with me."

Kirill's control snapped. Holding Andrei by the hair, he bent his head back and leaned over him. "Get up, take your pants off, and lean over my desk."

The grin on Andrei's face told him that had been exactly what he wanted. Andrei stood and had his pants around his ankles in a couple of seconds. When he leaned over the table, Kirill got another surprise.

"Fuck." Kirill gripped the base of his cock and squeezed.

Andrei winked at him over his shoulder. "I'm all stretched and prepped for you, love." He wriggled his ass.

Kirill slid one hand under his mate's thin shirt, admiring the play of muscle under his smooth skin. With his other hand, he grabbed the base of the black plug peeking from Andrei's hole.

Andrei grunted, his back straining when Kirill wriggled the plug. "Please."

"A begging alpha," Kirill mused. "I love you so damn much. By the way . . ." He carefully worked the plug out and placed it on his desk. He rubbed his thumb over the stretched rim of Andrei's hole. "What mysterious appointment in my day planner were you talking about?"

"Ultrasound."

Kirill paused in slathering his dick with lube. "What?"

Andrei gasped. "Fuck. Me."

Moaning, Kirill placed his cock head against Andrei's pucker and entered him with one hard, deep thrust. His eyes rolled back in his head from Andrei's heat, so tight and perfect around him. He clutched Andrei's hips and set a pace of hard, fast strokes. Andrei's gasps and moans, and the sound of his pelvis slapping against Andrei's ass, combined to form a symphony of passion and lust.

Kirill slid his hand up Andrei's back. He pushed the shirt up under his pits in the process and tangled his fingers in his hair again, holding on tight as he pummeled Andrei's ass. "Love your distraction techniques."

"Fuck . . . Kirill." Andrei braced his hands against the desk and forcefully pushed his hips back. "Been so long. Make me come! *Touch* me."

Kirill bent over Andrei's back and reached around him, fisting his heavy, hot prick. He wasn't gentle as he stroked Andrei's shaft. He knew Andrei liked it rough whenever he gave in to the urge of bottoming for Kirill.

"Yes!" A hard shudder ran through Andrei's strong body. "Harder! Come on. *Own* me. Show me who I belong to."

Snarling, Kirill slid his free hand over Andrei's hairy chest and pinched one of his nipples. He pumped his hips harder and, at the same time, bit Andrei's shoulder—not hard enough to break skin, but it would sting nonetheless.

That was all it took for Andrei to scream his name. His channel tightened with painful intensity around Kirill's dick and wrenched a toe-curling, teeth-clenching orgasm from him. Kirill grunted as he filled Andrei with jets of cum. He stroked Andrei through his own release, loving how Andrei's cock twitched and shot in his hand. He'd probably splattered all over the desk.

Huffing for breath, Kirill loosened his hold on Andrei's shoulder and rested his cheek on Andrei's back. "Damn. Needed that."

Andrei hummed. He reached back and placed his big hand on Kirill's hip, stroking him softly. "Me too. Louis will be glad I got laid."

"The fuck?" Kirill snarled. "What does Louis have to do with our sex life?" The beta had no business thinking about Andrei and sex, period. Kirill had gotten along with Louis pretty well right from the start, considering as alpha mate he held a higher position but didn't have as much say-so as the clan's beta. Maybe he needed to have a talk with Louis.

Andrei laughed, the movement causing Kirill's dick to slip from his ass. He lifted up on his elbows and looked over his shoulder. "Poor Louis is sore as hell from the daily training sessions I put him through. Without you wearing me out every night, I have too much energy. It has to go somewhere, so my enforcers and Louis have to bear the brunt of it. Today he yelled at me and told me to get laid before I killed one of them."

Kirill snorted. He slapped Andrei's well-rounded ass before he fell back in his chair, not bothering to cover his soft prick. They'd been loud enough to warn everyone in the house not to bother them. "Glad I can make our beta happy." He yanked his shirt over his head and cleaned his hand and groin area.

Andrei straightened and stretched his arms. He laughed, a flush covering his cheeks over his dark beard, as he nudged the papers on Kirill's desk. "Haley will kill me. I might've ruined her color schemes."

Groaning, Kirill threw his shirt at Andrei who caught it with one hand. "Are you kidding me? She's on a warpath anyway." He fixed his pants, stood, and stepped beside Andrei. Kirill lifted one sheet of paper and grimaced at the mess. "Fuck. That *will* be hard to explain."

Andrei rubbed Kirill's shirt over his cock and through his crease. "Nah. It was obvious I was gonna ravish you the moment I entered this office."

Kirill collected the ruined pages and tossed them in the trash. "Huh. One page survived our shenanigans. Guess we worked out a color scheme in our own unique way."

"What did I tell you?" Andrei kissed his cheek, then reached down, pulled up his pants, and closed the zipper. "With love and courage, we'll nail this clan business."

Kirill threw back his head and laughed, sinking against Andrei's taller, broader frame. He looped his arms around Andrei and snuggled in, enjoying the scent of sweat and sex clinging to his skin. "I love you."

Andrei kissed his forehead. "Love you more. But we need to leave if we want to make it in time."

"Right. Ultrasound. I totally forgot." Paw's Cove had no shifter doctor, so they had to go to Hazel Woods and see Doctor Ian Albright. Mary was supposed to give birth in four to five weeks.

"Mary's waiting for us." Andrei rubbed his hand down his side, then stood back and held out his palm.

Kirill took it and followed Andrei out of his office.

CHAPTER TWO

A ndrei squeezed Kirill's hand as he stared at the black-and-white picture on the monitor, fighting tears of joy. A quick glance at his mate showed Kirill was in a similar predicament.

Mary chuckled and drew Andrei's attention. "You two are insanely cute. My ex-husband wasn't nearly as enthusiastic about our little ones."

"Because he was a prick," Andrei muttered. When his cousin Mary had called him last year to tell him Gene had divorced her and left her alone with four cubs, he'd immediately offered his help. He'd paid for her move and given her a house on clan lands. As a thank-you, she'd expressed her wish to make Andrei and Kirill's biggest dream come true.

Kirill took Mary's hand and leaned over to press a kiss to her long black hair. "You are a gem. I can't wait to be a daddy and hold our little honey cookie. And I love that he or she will grow up with so many cousins."

Andrei rubbed Kirill's back and concentrated on the ultrasound again. This close to the birthing date, he was able to make out the baby's head, rump, and limbs quite clearly. It was damn exciting.

Doctor Albright moved the wand over Mary's huge belly, a tender smile on his face. "The baby has a strong heartbeat and is perfectly normal in size. Are you sure you don't want to know the gender?"

"We want it to be a surprise." Andrei met Ian's gaze. "Kirill hates gender coloring anyway, so he painted the nursery in soft greens." The shades Kirill had chosen made for a stunning set-up when combined with the white furniture Kirill's father had bought for them.

Mary nodded. "And Kirill and I went out and shopped for a ton of green, red, yellow, and orange baby clothes."

Andrei smiled as he remembered a cute onesie Kirill had shown him last week. It was bright yellow with a print of a cartoon bear and the words *Papa Bear's Favorite.*

Ian took some measurements and noted them in the baby's file. "Four more weeks and you'll finally hold your precious. Are you glad it's only one?" He smirked. "I remember Shea's reaction when he saw his triplets for the first time. Poor guy's face switched from white to green and back again. Thank Fate he had Viktor."

Kirill nodded. "As much as I want to be a father, I couldn't cope with three cubs at the same time. Don't know how Shea and Dad do it."

"Especially now Stefan's mated and doesn't have as much time anymore," Andrei said. "Hey, Mary. Are up for a visit with Viktor and Shea?"

Mary hummed while Ian cleaned her belly. "Honestly, I'm tired. Maybe another day?"

A knock sounded, and a moment later Ian's mate, Rose, opened the door to the exam room. "Darling? I got a call from Kyle Andrews over in Paw's Cove. His stubborn father fell off a ladder trying to fix the roof. He's afraid the old guy might have a concussion." She winked at Andrei. "Second time this month."

"Awesome." Ian snapped his latex gloves off. "Mary, if you want, I can take you home so Kirill can go and see his dads." He stood and pressed a couple of buttons on the ultrasound machine. It whirred for a moment. Ian snatched the picture of their baby and handed it to Kirill.

Mary straightened her dress. "Thank you, Ian. That would

be lovely." When she held out her hand, Andrei took it. He placed his arm under her back and helped her from the exam couch. She touched his chest, smiling happily. "Don't look so worried, Andrei. I've been through this before, remember? I feel fine. I'll let Ian take me home, take a nap, then pester someone for a meal."

Andrei suppressed a snort. He suspected Mary had a thing for one of his enforcers, or maybe even Louis, but he wasn't sure yet if anyone returned her feelings. "Sounds like a plan. But you'll call me or Ian if you feel as though anything's wrong."

"Sure, cuz." She patted his cheek—a little too hard—and waddled toward Rose. "While Ian gets ready, I'd love to hear the latest Hazel Woods news. Is it true Phoenix threatened to toss Adrianna out of the clan?" The two women left the room, chattering quietly.

Andrei shot Kirill a questioning look, but Kirill shrugged.

"My mate is the biggest gossip." Although Ian sighed, the lovey-dovey look on his face told Andrei he didn't mind Rose's hobby too much.

Kirill nudged him in the side. "Come on, love. Let's see what the dads are up to. Maybe they'll let us stay for dinner."

"Dinner?" It was only two. "What aren't you telling me?"

A blush spread over Kirill's pale features. "I may have an appointment with Haley at four. She wants to discuss the order of songs that'll be played by the band during the Harvest Festival."

Andrei laughed. "You're a sneaky fucker."

Viktor's house should've been a place of chaos and destruction, given that three cubs were simultaneously learning to walk, talk, and throw things all the time. But the place was pristine as ever, though littered with toys. Andrei sat on the sofa with Tara, who chewed on a teething ring, perched on his lap. She'd cried earlier because her gums obviously hurt, but she'd calmed down once Andrei picked her up and threw her in the air a couple of times.

Shea sat beside him and ate a banana, a sleeping Noah in his arms. The little one had dropped like a stone after playing with Uncle Kirill. Kirill was on the rug before the fireplace, stacking blocks with a wide-eyed Georgia.

"Kil," she said, handing Kirill a red block with her chubby hand.

Shea smiled indulgently. "Thanks for coming. Viktor's busy in his office, going over some stuff with Phoenix and Juri. Miss Teething was driving her siblings crazy before you dropped by. I didn't know who to console first. Georgia lost her patience and started throwing her blocks at Tara. Noah was in the way, and I managed to snatch him before he was clocked in the head."

"Mary had an appointment today, so we took full advantage. I know how much Kirill misses seeing you all on a daily basis. He's been awfully busy."

Shea smirked. "Trying to impress the clan, I'd wager. It's important to take breaks, or he'll burn out. Admittedly, I didn't have much time to grow into the alpha mate role before Viktor stepped back. But I see Juri doing the same thing, although he's lived in Hazel Woods all his life. Phoenix had to remind him the clan loves him already without his having to prove his worth."

Andrei hummed, kissing Tara's fluffy brown hair. "Rose mentioned something earlier. Trouble between Phoenix and Adrianna?" Phoenix had taken over leadership of the clan the past winter after a challenge to Juri, Viktor's oldest son. Although Juri had lost the challenge, he'd found his mate in Phoenix.

Shea sighed. "Adrianna." Her name fell from his lips like a curse. No surprise there, since she was Viktor's ex-wife and the mother of Juri, Stefan, and Kirill. "She and Hetty Taft set out to slander Devin."

Kirill looked up from his fight with Georgia over a green block. "Hetty? The waitress from the diner?"

Shea nodded. "She had a run-in with Devin and his kids before he got together with Stefan. She was rude, accused him of not being able to care for his kids because he was a single omega."

"What a bitter old hag." Andrei gently rubbed Tara's chubby leg. "Everyone knows what a devoted father Devin is."

Placing Noah against his shoulder, Shea leaned toward the side table and disposed of his banana peel. "Well, Adrianna is a friend of hers. The two women informed shifter child service."

"What the—" Kirill broke off with a quick glance at Georgia. He relinquished his hold on the block and ruffled her hair. "My mother called child service on her own son-in-law?"

"Yeah. Apparently, she was against Stefan and Devin's mating. Thought she'd kill two birds with one stone. Stefan was livid when he found out. Devin had given birth to their third child the day before when child services dropped by unannounced. Stefan isn't Tommy and Beth's biological father, but he loves them just the same. He immediately hurried over here to get Viktor's help. Crashed a meeting between Phoenix, Viktor, and another alpha from a wolf pack." Shea snickered. "It was quite exciting. The last time I saw Vik so mad, your enforcer had attacked Kirill."

Andrei winced, remembering the incident. "Damn. What happened then?"

Kirill was playing with Georgia, but his focus was on their conversation. His cheeks were red, probably with anger.

"Phoenix ordered Hetty and Adrianna to his office while

Viktor went and talked to the lady from child service. Nothing could've kept him from protecting Devin and his grandkids. Ours, I mean, though I still think I'm too young to be a gramps at twenty-six." Shea rubbed Noah's tiny back in circles, pushed his nose against the baby's neck, and breathed deeply.

"Will Phoenix give her the boot or not?" Kirill asked.

"I sure hope so," a gruff voice said.

Andrei looked up to find Devin in the doorway. He held Tommy's hand, and Beth was perched on his hip. Beth was a month older than Shea's triplets, and when she saw Georgia, she squealed and stretched her arms in her direction. "Dada!"

"What is it, sweetie?" Stefan came up behind Devin, looking out of breath. He held a car seat with a sleeping baby. "Oh, hey guys." He gave a wave when he saw them. "Andrei. Didn't know you were here."

Kirill stood and relieved Devin of Beth. "Spontaneous idea. Tommy, do you want to come play with your sister and Georgia?" When the boy nodded enthusiastically and let go of his father's hand, Kirill took both kids to the rug. He sat Beth beside Georgia.

Georgia laughed and offered one of her blocks. "Bet."

Stefan flopped down beside Andrei on the sofa, placing the car seat between his feet. "It's good to see you." He bent over and freed his son from the seat. He lifted the baby against his chest and kissed his head. The boy shuffled and yawned, blinking his blue eyes open.

"Hey, little Dimitri." Andrei softly touched Dimitri's cheek. "Shea's telling me about your trouble with Adrianna. Anything I can do to help?"

Stefan's features darkened. "She totally fu . . . dged up her chances to ever spend time with her grandkids. I'll never let her near my family after the stunt she pulled. Phoenix is dealing with her."

"Understandable," Kirill said. "She won't be invited to the baby shower."

Andrei frowned. "The what?"

Kirill waved his hand. "Ask Haley." He returned his attention back to Devin, who sat in an armchair, and the two chatted quietly.

Andrei met Stefan's gaze. "I'm sorry she's causing so much trouble."

Stefan grinned. "Let's switch children. You can use the practice. It'll be a while before you have to worry about teething and tantrums."

It took a bit of careful juggling, but Andrei and Stefan managed to relocate Tara to his lap and Dimitri into Andrei's arms. "He's so tiny." He kissed the boy's fingers when he reached for Andrei's beard. Dimitri had been born a month ago. Andrei loved his sweet baby scent and nuzzled his surprisingly thick blond hair. Dimitri grunted and ruffled his tiny fingers through Andrei's beard. "And quite the charmer."

"Just like his dad," Stefan said, a warm smile on his face.

"Papa." Tommy came running and stopped beside the sofa. He placed his hands on Stefan's thigh and bounced on his toes. "Daddy said Uncle Andrei and Uncle Kirill will have a baby soon. Can we go and see it?"

Stefan laughed. "In another month, yes." He focused on Andrei. "How's Mary?"

"Not half as nervous as Kirill and me. Here . . ." Andrei peeled the picture from his pocket and held it up for Stefan. "Our baby." He grinned when Tommy craned his neck and handed the boy the picture.

Tommy's eyes widened. "Looks like the pictures of Beth and Dimi on the fridge. Is it a boy or a girl?" He crawled on the couch between Andrei and Stefan, dangling his legs.

"We don't know." Andrei winced when Dimitri tried to

stab his eye with a tiny finger. He placed his hand gently around the tyke's hand. "It's a surprise."

Tommy grinned up at him. "You need cake when the baby comes. We had cake for Dimi." His head suddenly snapped around, then he shouted and jumped off the couch. "Pappy!"

Viktor stopped in the doorway, went down to one knee, and opened his arms. Tommy flung himself at him. Laughing, Viktor stood and whirled the boy around. "Hey Tommy."

"Can we go out and play with your bear, Pappy?"

Andrei leaned toward Shea and muttered, "What does he call you?"

"Sheppy." Shea rolled his eyes. "It's kinda cute. We're the first grandparents to really pay attention to him. Hey, how about you all stay for dinner?" Shea's eyes sparkled. "It's not often we have the whole family under one roof. I want to feed and spoil you."

Viktor walked over and leaned down to kiss Shea on the lips, Tommy still clinging to him like a limpet. "Wonderful idea, love."

Kirill pumped his fist in the air. "Yes!" If his expression held some guilt, only Andrei knew the reason.

CHAPTER THREE

"Is this necessary? I don't think I'm in any danger." Kirill took in the many women, men, and children milling around the town square of Paw's Cove. Clan members had grouped beside the stage, putting together a garland made of oak leaf clusters, rowanberries, and faux green silk. Haley had been happy when Kirill had handed her the one color scheme Andrei hadn't ruined. Bright green, ruby, and tan were the official Harvest Feast colors.

On the other side of the stage, three men heaved pumpkins from a trailer attached to a tractor. Children sat at a long picnic table, crafting stuff out of chestnuts and acorns.

Kirill started out of his reverie when Louis nudged him and pointed. He followed the direction he indicated and tensed.

"Are you *sure* you're not in danger?" Louis snickered.

"Kirill," Haley called out to him, raising her arm. As though he had any chance of missing her in this crowd.

Kirill whirled around to Louis and fisted the beta's sweatshirt with both hands. "Help me. It's your duty to protect the alpha mate. Prove you're worth your huge salary."

Louis cocked one eyebrow. "Beta is an honorary position and *has* no salary. Well, I do live in my house for free, but I also have a regular job—"

"Drivel." He slapped Louis' chest. The guy was as tall and broad as Andrei. "Go and distract her before she's on me. If she asks me one more time to assess the marching band's costumes, I'll run away screaming. Flirt with her if you have to."

Louis coughed. Pink stained his cheeks. "Actually, I'm

kinda bisexual. And ever since Andrei came out to us and mated with you, I've been hoping to . . . date a guy. I never—"

"Oh, for fuck's sake." Kirill growled and gave Louis his back. "You're good for nothing." He raised his voice. "Haley, hey. Looks good, huh? Do you still need me around? I thought"—he checked his watch—"I'd go and see if Mary needs anything."

Haley narrowed her eyes, her lips pressed into a thin line. Stopping before him, she placed one hand on her hip. She held a clipboard in her other hand. A pencil stuck out of the messy bun on her head. "Kirill Vasiliev."

"Bazin," he reminded her. "Changed my name so Andrei, the baby, and I will have the same surname." Kirill hoped that would distract her from harassing him with something he had to do. *Please, don't let it be the marching band.*

She rolled her eyes. "Yeah, whatever. I need you to come with me and talk with Hester. He complained about the order of songs we decided on."

Hester was the band's boss. And not *they* had decided on the order, Haley had done it because he'd ditched her the day he and Andrei had had dinner at his dads' house. He was sure reminding her wouldn't win him any sympathy.

She rattled on. "And you have to talk with the women in the band. Some of them don't want to wear skirts." She huffed. "They actually accused me of being sexist. Can you believe it?"

Kirill shot Louis a begging look, but the useless lug shrugged his shoulders and held up his hands. *Traitor.* Kirill sighed deeply and scratched his hair. "Haley, I don't see the problem. As long as everyone's dressed, I don't care if they wear a skirt or pants, be they man or woman. Don't be so stuffy. This is a festival, a cause of celebrating our great town where everyone is welcome regardless of gender identity, color, ethnicity, religion, or sexual orientation."

Louis clapped his hands, a wide grin on his face. "Awesome, Kirill. I think that's a perfect closing sentence for your big speech."

"My what now?" Kirill turned to him, squinting. When Louis' grin fell and his mocha skin paled, Kirill lowered his voice to a deep growl. "Haley?"

"Of course you'll give a speech. Didn't Andrei tell you? I asked him to do it, but he said you'd be much better suited." Haley sounded pissed. "And I'm not stuffy. You know what? Take care of everything on your own if you're such an expert on Paw's Cove." She slapped the clipboard against his chest, turned, and marched off.

Kirill shook his head. "What the fuck's wrong with her?"

Louis pursed his lips. "She's jealous because you're alpha mate, a title she's salivated over since her father handed the reigns to Andrei. Haley thought mating with Andrei was her birthright. Good thing Andrei didn't agree. He'd have been miserable as hell. I've never seen him happier than when he's with you."

"But . . ." Kirill pinched the bridge of his nose. "I thought she encouraged Andrei to be true to himself."

Louis snorted. "Yeah, right. You see how she went overboard with the Harvest Festival? She had two folders prepared for her mating ceremony and wedding with Andrei before he ever set foot in Paw's Cove."

"Crazy." Kirill sighed. "And now I have to stay and plan this shindig all alone because she took off. Fuck." He glanced around him, watching all those people who relied on him. He was the fucking alpha mate. He couldn't let them down.

Louis cleared his throat. "Are you sure the men should stack the pumpkins so messily? Maybe if we . . ." Louis trailed off, blushing harder when Kirill looked at him. "What?"

"Louis, my man, you just got yourself a promotion. You're

now my personal assistant." Ignoring Louis' panicked expression, Kirill slapped his beefy shoulder, then grabbed him by his sweater and dragged him toward the stage. "You're on pumpkin-stacking duty. Make me proud."

CHAPTER FOUR

"Welcome, Desmond." Andrei reached over his desk and shook the tall man's hand. "Normally, Kirill would be with me to greet a potential new member, but he's busy with the planning for the Paw's Cove Harvest Festival and Feast. The whole town celebrates its founding. And of course it's harvest season. Pumpkin-spiced everything." He shrugged.

Desmond grinned as he took a seat. "Sounds like a huge celebration. I'm looking forward to it. After spending over a decade in the city, I'd love a nice and easy party in the country."

Andrei coughed as he remembered Haley's big plans. Nothing *easy* there. He studied Desmond. The grizzly bear shifter stood six three, with wide shoulders and a little extra padding around the middle. His dirty blond hair reached to his collar, and intelligent brown eyes twinkled with a heavy dose of happiness. Andrei had no doubt Desmond, who was forty and divorced, would fit right in. He had an open, easygoing personality.

"I admit I picked Paw's Cove specifically because of you. Heard about your choice of mate and . . ." Desmond shrugged.

Arching a brow, Andrei drummed his fingers on his desk. "Phoenix Jones over in Hazel Woods is also mated to a man."

"True. But he only took over last year." Desmond floated his flat palm in the air. "Wasn't sure of him."

"He's kinda my brother-in-law and a great guy." Andrei laughed. He skimmed over the application Desmond had sent a month earlier. "Seeing as Paw's Cove is in desperate need of a fire chief, and you'd be perfect for the position, I won't complain 'cause you chose my clan. Nobody will hassle you for your choice of partner. My mate took great care in weeding out the homophobes."

Desmond sighed, his shoulders relaxing visibly. "Good to know. My ex was understandably pissed when she found out I prefer the company of men. I gave in to pressure when I was younger, followed my father's orders. So, any cute single guys in Paw's Cove?"

Andrei laughed. "Probably. Kirill will know them better than I do because they confide in him. The Harvest Festival will be a great opportunity to get to know someone. As soon as the beer flows, inhibitions lower, and one or more guys might be inclined to . . . explore."

"I'm actually looking for something serious instead of a man who wants a walk on the wild side." Desmond hummed. "I'll find him. My mom said it was like lightning struck her when she met my father. A gut feeling."

"Well—excuse me." Andrei grabbed his cell and swiped over the display. He had a message from Kirill. "My mate," he explained as he opened the message.

A speech? You're a dead man, Bazin. When I come home, you better wait for me with your ass lubed and up in the air.

Andrei swallowed around the sudden lump in his throat. His ears felt hot, and he quickly reached up and scratched one. Andrei had totally blocked out that particular conversation with Haley. He wriggled in his chair.

"Bad news?" Desmond asked. "Do you need to leave?"

"Uh." Clearing his throat, Andrei placed his cell on the desk. "Nah. Just . . . Kirill teasing me. He found out about a surprise."

Desmond grinned, looking too smug for Andrei's liking. He jumped when the door was pushed open so hard it smashed against the wall and repelled. Desmond growled.

"Excuse me, lady? This is a private conversation."

Andrei stood. "Haley, you'll show some respect and knock on my fucking door before you enter." When she didn't look sorry, he growled a warning.

Haley's cheeks were red. Several strands of hair had escaped her bun. The top she was wearing under her open blouse had slid down and allowed a peek at her pink bra. To a straight guy, she probably would have looked enticing.

Desmond stared at her with something like bored annoyance.

"Haley? I'm waiting for an explanation." Andrei crossed his arms over his chest.

She pouted. "I have a complaint concerning your mate, Alpha." She stomped her foot. "He said I'm stuffy because I didn't want to give in to the marching band's demands. After all I've done for the festival, he had the audacity to tell me I'm doing it *wrong*. *Me*? I've planned this festival since my daddy—"

Andrei raised his hand, stopping her rambling. "It was my impression Kirill was responsible for planning the festival. You're assisting him."

She snorted. "Assisting? Nothing would be ready in time if I left the planning to Kirill. He's absolutely inefficient and lazy, and he lacks the skills needed to host something as important as the Paw's Cove Harvest Festival and Feast."

Growling deep in his chest, Andrei left his spot behind his desk and walked toward her. "You have the guts to call my mate lazy? After he's put in fourteen-hour days over the past few weeks to not only keep up with his usual duties but to help with the festival as well? Where's Kirill now?"

Haley avoided his gaze. "At the town square with Louis. Most likely fucking up what I've worked my fingers bloody for."

"Interesting. As far as I know, you live with your mom.

You don't have a job, since Francine from the Beauty Salon fired you for repeatedly turning up late. Your sole job for the clan has been assisting with the festival organization. So you left my beta and mate, who have a hell of a lot more to do than you do, to fend for themselves while you come to me with your stupid tantrum? Your complaint is hereby dismissed."

Haley gaped at him. "You can't be serious! I'm the former alpha's daughter. You can't treat me—"

"I'm treating you like a clan member who's slandering my mate out of jealousy." Andrei flexed his muscles. "Don't think I haven't noticed."

Desmond whistled quietly. "Damn. Look at her. If looks could kill. Guess you hit that nail on the head."

"Oh, fuck you," Haley spat out. She fixed Andrei with a heated glare. "When you mated Kirill, I knew you'd need an heir someday. I thought you'd at least consider me as a surrogate. But no, you had to bring your cousin into the mix. I would've been a good mother."

Andrei frowned. "Why would I want a mother for my and Kirill's child? Why would I want you to give birth to Kirill's baby?"

Haley let out a screech. "Because two men can't raise a cub, you stupid prick! Of course the kid needs a mom. Me! I should've carried *your* seed and become the mother of the next alpha, as my father promised. What the hell would a queer like Kirill want with a cub anyway?"

Andrei trembled with barely contained anger. He fought the urge to wrap his hands around Haley's neck. He'd known about her jealousy, but how had he not seen how much she hated Kirill? He wondered if Kirill had seen it coming.

Desmond stood and placed a hand on his shoulder. "Alpha, take a deep breath before you kill her," he murmured.

Haley's eyes widened, and the angry red color on her face gave way to a pasty white. She took a couple steps back.

Andrei flexed his hands. "Haley, you're hereby banished from the Paw's Cove clan."

She gasped. "What? No! I was born here. You can't take my home from me."

"You may stay in town if you wish, but you're no longer welcome at clan functions. Including the Harvest Festival. And you'll stay away from Kirill, Mary, and any of my future children." Andrei lowered his voice. "If you go against my orders, Louis will forcefully remove you from the clan's premises."

Haley wobbled. "Yes, Alpha," she whispered.

Andrei opened the office door and called for an enforcer. "Colin! I want you to escort Haley to her mother's house." He sighed and focused back on Desmond. "It's not always so exciting. Would you like to have dinner with me and Kirill today? I want to introduce you. Welcome to Paw's Cove." He held out his hand and smiled when Desmond shook it.

It was obvious Andrei hadn't followed through on Kirill's demand as soon as he and Louis stepped through the door. Kirill heard Andrei and another man chatting animatedly. "Let's see what my guy's up to, Louis. He better not be flirting with someone, or his ass will never recover."

A coughing fit shook Louis, but he followed Kirill to the kitchen.

Andrei stood at the stove, stirring something in a pot, while a strange blond man leaned against the kitchen island, a glass of wine in his hand. When the stranger looked up, his eyes widened. He took in first Louis, then Kirill, before he turned his attention back to Louis. His cheeks flushed red.

"Andrei," the man whispered. "Please tell me the god with the mocha skin is *not* your mate."

Andrei whirled around. A smile spread over his face as

soon as he saw Kirill. "Hey, honey muffin. I made dinner." He dried his hands on a dishtowel and hurried over, pulling Kirill into a tight hug.

"Oh, thank fuck," the stranger muttered.

Kirill frowned as he met Andrei's gaze. "Babe? Who's the drooling man in our kitchen? And why didn't you follow my orders?"

Andrei laughed, turned them, and urged him toward the stranger. "Kirill, I'd like you to meet Desmond Wilkins. He applied to join the clan and he would like the open position of fire chief. I invited him for dinner because I can't accept him without your okay." Andrei grinned. "Desmond, this is my Kirill, the love of my life."

Kirill melted. How could he stay mad at Andrei when he was in such a sweet mood? Kirill held out his hand to Desmond. "Nice to meet you. But I guess you'd rather talk with Louis than with me." He laughed.

Desmond looked past Kirill while he shook his hand. "Louis," he said breathily. He let go of Kirill's hand and walked around him and Andrei. Coming to stop right in front of Louis, he reached out tentatively and hooked his index finger around Louis'. "Hi. I . . . I'm Desmond. You're gorgeous. Please tell me you're single and searching."

Louis eyes were wide. "Uh . . . are you always this straight-forward?"

"Yes. I mean . . . no. Only . . . I've never been so instantly attracted to anyone before. Gut feeling." Desmond reached up as if to cup Louis' face, but the beta pulled away.

"Whoa." Louis frowned. "Calm down, tiger. I don't know you."

"Right. Of course." Desmond scratched through his thick blond hair. He lowered his gaze to the floor and shuffled his feet. "If you don't have a date for the Harvest Festival, I'd be honored to be yours. Please?"

Kirill grinned and looked up at Andrei. "That's so cute," he whispered. "Have you ever seen two huge men blush and fumble for words like this?"

Andrei embraced him from behind and placed his chin on Kirill's shoulder. "Is Louis interested in . . ."

"He's bi but looking for a man." Kirill snuggled under Andrei's arm. "Smells good in here. What did you prepare for dinner?"

"I can hear you, you know? Bear shifter." Louis sounded disgruntled.

Andrei smirked. "Spaghetti and meat balls."

Louis groaned. "My favorite. Fine." He grabbed the fabric over the middle of Desmond's chest and pulled him toward the kitchen table. "We can sit, eat, and get to know each other over a glass of wine. If I still like you by the end of dinner, I'll be your date for the festival."

Desmond followed Louis with a besotted look on his face.

Kirill briefly pushed his ass into the cradle of Andrei's groin. "Your punishment is postponed, not cancelled."

"Lucky me," Andrei quipped.

CHAPTER FIVE

Andrei woke to hot suction around his prick. Placing an arm over his eyes, he groaned and reached down with his free hand. He tangled his fingers in Kirill's soft hair and stroked through the strands. "I love you."

Kirill hummed around him, sending Andrei's senses reeling. Gasping for breath, he lifted his hips to seek more of the delicious heat that was Kirill's mouth. Kirill placed one strong arm over Andrei's hips and pressed him down on the bed.

"Baby . . . please." Andrei wasn't sure what he was begging for. His mate gave the best blow jobs, so he was a happy bear. Letting go of Kirill's hair, he lifted on his elbows and watched his dick disappear and reappear between Kirill's plush pink lips. "Fuck, what a pretty sight. I'll never tire of watching you."

Kirill winked. He cupped Andrei's balls and rolled them gently. He gave them a soft squeeze, then sucked Andrei's cock to the base.

Trembling under the sensuous onslaught, Andrei hissed. "Yes! I love how you can take all of me." Not an easy feat, considering his size. He grunted when Kirill swallowed repeatedly around his crown. When Kirill trailed his sneaky fingers from his balls down to his crease, Andrei spread his legs wider. He panted in anticipation while he waited for Kirill's digits to breach him.

Andrei was the undisputed alpha of their clan, and Kirill was the perfect encouraging alpha mate and advisor, but still mostly defiant. In the privacy of their bedroom, stereotypes didn't exist. He wasn't the only alpha who enjoyed a pounding. After a few too many beers, Phoenix Jones had admitted to Andrei he almost exclusively bottomed for Juri.

Kirill let go of his dick with an obscene wet sound. "What are you thinking about?" He licked his shiny red lips.

"Uh . . . Phoenix."

"What?" Kirill's brown eyes turned to a bright sherry color. Growling, he pushed two fingers through the tight muscle guarding Andrei's channel.

Andrei flopped down on the bed and cursed. Whimpering and wriggling, he pushed down on the hard intrusion. When Kirill nudged his prostate, Andrei was close. He gasped when Kirill circled the base of his shaft with his thumb and index finger. "Babe?"

Kirill's eyes were tiny slits. "You think about other men while we're in bed? I shouldn't have let you off so easily last night."

Right. The punishment. Andrei had wheedled himself out of the mess with the speech by promising Kirill he'd give the damn thing as long as Kirill helped him write it. "I . . . um . . . sorry. I wasn't thinking of him as in . . . you know." He cursed when Kirill tightened the circle around his dick.

"You mean you weren't thinking of him as a fuckable man?" Kirill arched one eyebrow. "You won't shimmy out of trouble with sweet promises, not this time." He let go of Andrei's dick and rolled out of bed.

Momentarily befuddled and fighting against an orgasm when his lonely cock slapped against his own belly without Kirill's hold, Andrei squeezed his eyes closed. "Baby?" He snapped them open and followed Kirill's movements with his gaze. "Honey crumble?" He didn't care that his voice took on a desperate ring. What the hell was Kirill doing? "Why . . . are you leaving me like this?" He waved down to his painfully hard prick.

Kirill threw him a look over his shoulder before he vanished in the bathroom, leaving the door open. "Like I said, you deserve a punishment. No coming for now."

Groaning, Andrei fell back on the mattress. "You can't be serious! This shit hurts." He slid one hand down his belly, intending to grab himself.

"I know. And don't even think about beating off."

Andrei's focus snapped from his dick to the bathroom door. "I wasn't!" He bit his tongue. Hell and damnation, but he understood why Kirill was mad. Andrei let out a desperate laugh and sat up, dangling his legs over the edge of the mattress. "You're a cruel man."

"Yes. Out of bed with you and get dressed. You have a speech to give." Kirill popped his head around the doorframe. "On a stage." He smirked. "In front of the whole town."

Andrei shook his head. "Evil bastard." He lowered his gaze between his legs. "You better make me think of something really disgusting, or I won't fit in my pants. Can't walk around with a boner all day, babe. It's a family friendly festival."

"What about Haley thinking she'll give birth to your cubs?"

Andrei shuddered.

Andrei tugged his sweater down over his groin and shifted from one foot to the other. Kirill was out to kill him. The bastard stood beside Louis, listening to the beta explaining the festival's procedure one last time, while he slid the fork into his mouth. Kirill hummed around the morsel of pumpkin pie as he slowly dragged the fork back through his plush lips.

"So, first Andrei's speech. Then the marching band with the first three songs, followed by the judging of the biggest pumpkin." Kirill nodded. "Sounds good. What do you think, darling?"

Andrei coughed into his fist. "I think I need at least five

minutes alone with you before the speech. Honestly, babe. The way you eat pie should be outlawed."

Kirill and Louis guffawed, but suddenly the humor slid from Louis' face and panic settled in. "Fuck. Me."

Andrei looked over his shoulder. He grinned when he saw Desmond swaggering toward their group with confidence. "I bet he'd love to, Louis. He's a man on a mission."

Louis whimpered. "I know I said we don't know each other, but his confidence is so sexy," he whispered. "I want to lick him from head to toe. But at the same time I'm scared shitless. Betas aren't supposed to be afraid of anything."

Kirill snorted. "Nonsense. It's perfectly normal to be nervous when you meet someone special."

Desmond had reached them and maneuvered around Kirill, sweeping Louis into his arms. "Hey, sweetheart. Ready for our date?"

Groaning, Louis grabbed the lapels of Desmond's light jacket and yanked him down for a kiss.

Andrei wrapped his arm around Kirill and led his staring mate away from the necking couple. "Let's give them some privacy. Do you think we have enough time to sneak behind the stage and —"

Kirill shook his head as he slid the tines of his fork through the pumpkin pie a clan member had given him before the official opening of the festival. Obviously, it wasn't only Andrei who was helpless against those begging brown eyes. "No hanky-panky, Alpha. You go up on the stage before the masses stir up a mutiny." He lifted the forked morsel and held it to Andrei's lips. "The guests want pie. They want the marching band and bobbing for apples and —"

"You've grown attached to our lovely festival since I removed Haley from the picture." Andrei snatched the bite and moaned when the flavors burst on his tongue. "Damn, this is good." He grimaced when he saw a woman eye them and the pie hungrily. "You're right. It's time I start this shindig. Hey, there's Mary." Andrei waved and led Kirill toward her. She stood in the first row before the stage with one of his enforcers, and he noticed the man had his hand on her back.

"Are Colin and Mary a thing?" Kirill whispered. "I'm glad she's not after Louis anymore."

"Colin might only feel protective of her in such a huge crowd since she's so close to giving birth." Andrei shrugged. Colin had to be at least ten years younger than Mary, who came with four kids and baggage.

When Andrei and Kirill stopped beside them, Colin pulled himself to his full height and puffed out his chest. "Alpha." He dipped his head respectfully. "Mary is safe with me. You have my word."

Andrei clapped him on the shoulder, then leaned down and kissed Mary's rosy cheek. "I have no doubt. That healthy glow on your face suits you, cousin." He winked. "I have a speech to give, but I'd love to catch up with you after. Kirill, come with me?"

"Of course." Kirill took his hand and dragged him to the side of the stage and up the four steps.

Andrei grinned as he took in the town square decked out in the colors of fall. Kirill and the many volunteers had outdone themselves. The townsfolk clustered in groups around the booths offering grilled meats, pies, and beverages, chatting with friends and catching up on gossip. Children laughed and ran between the adults. Some of the smaller ones had congregated around a patch of pumpkins and were trying to climb the orange decoration. Andrei saw people waving at each other and embracing. The happiness all around was contagious, and he lifted Kirill's hand and pressed a kiss to his knuckles.

Stepping up to the microphone, Andrei tapped against it to garner everyone's attention. People—human and clan alike—

turned with smiles on their faces. Many of them waved at him and Kirill and they waved back. "Welcome to Paw's Cove's Harvest Festival and Feast!" Andrei paused when the people cheered. "First of all, a big thank you to all of you. The Harvest Festival has been a tradition since our lovely town was founded in 1895. Our big family is growing with every person who moves to Paw's Cove and enriches our heritage, so I'm sure we have many more years of celebrations to look forward to. This town is a safe place for everyone, no matter the color of their skin, ethnicity, origin, sexual orientation, or gender identity. Paw's Cove is as welcoming and colorful as its citizens." He squeezed Kirill's hand when people clapped.

Andrei saw some Pride flags in the crowd and knew he and Kirill had done the right thing when they'd admitted their feelings to each other last spring. It had been time to set an example. "I'd like to thank the volunteers who put in many many hours of their free time to help make today a success. And, of course" — he pulled Kirill against his side and cupped his cheek—"thank you, my wonderful mate, for organizing this day. I love you." Andrei dipped his head and kissed an obviously surprised Kirill.

Kirill clutched at his arms and melted against him while the crowd cheered and laughed. Andrei tasted Kirill's soft lips for a moment longer. However, when the cheers died down, a long, pained wail filled the silence.

Andrei whirled around and searched the crowd, immediately fixing his gaze on Colin, who had his arms around a red-faced Mary. People had backed away from her, and Andrei noticed the puddle under her. "Shit. Mary's water just broke."

Kirill gasped beside him. "No. It's two weeks too soon."

"Uh . . ." Andrei cleared his throat and spoke into the mic. "That said, have a great festival. Eat pie and be merry." Clinging to Kirill's hand, he dragged his mate off the stage. "Mary!"

She panted when they stopped beside her, holding onto

Colin's arms with a white-knuckled grip. "I'm fine, but we should go. I had one public birth when it was Bridgit's time. Not again."

Andrei looked around helplessly, breathing a sigh of relief when Desmond and Louis pushed through the crowd. "Louis, great. Can you go and fetch the midwife? I last saw Erin at the pumpkin patch, watching the little ones. Take her to our house."

Louis nodded and hurried off with Desmond in tow.

Colin swung a protesting Mary into his arms. "Alpha, your car?"

"Right. This way." Andrei slung his arm around an awfully pale Kirill.

"Two weeks," Kirill muttered under his breath, his eyes glassy.

Andrei laughed. "Honey, don't freak out on me. The baby's coming. I need you with me."

Kirill stared down into the tiny pink face of his daughter in disbelief. She was perfect, with her rosebud mouth and surprisingly long lashes. After a rushed birth and lots of screaming, she was sleeping peacefully in Kirill's arms.

Andrei sat beside him on the bed and carefully touched her tiny toes where her foot stuck out of the green blanket Erin had wrapped her in. The midwife and Mary had done an awesome job. Mary snored lightly beside them.

"She's the most beautiful thing I've ever seen," Kirill whispered. He was a father. The whole magnitude of his new responsibilities would probably hit him later, but for now he was just happy to hold her.

Andrei sniffled and placed his big hand around the baby's head. "Yeah. I love her so much. I love you both." He kissed Kirill's cheek. "Do you have a name for her?"

Kirill hummed. They had discussed names many times, but never found one they both liked. "What about Victoria?"

Andrei chuckled. "I love it. And your dad will walk around with a puffed-out chest for months." He bent and kissed Victoria's forehead. "Yeah, the name fits perfectly."

"I never thought I'd ever be this happy." Kirill blinked rapidly. "I found the love of my life, a new home, and now I have a family. Do you want more kids? I think we should have more." Although Juri and Stefan annoyed the fuck out of him sometimes, he'd also loved having brothers growing up. He wanted the same for Victoria. "She needs someone who'll steal her toys and cling to her when all she wants is to spend time with her cool friends."

Andrei arched one eyebrow. "I'm glad you have such a good relationship with your brothers. I don't know if Mary would be willing to go through another pregnancy. It was her fifth, after all." He nuzzled Kirill's temple. "Wait until Victoria wakes us up three times a night because she's hungry, wet, or generally displeased with something, and you'll forget about having a second one for a while."

"Maybe." Kirill wouldn't give up. He'd always wanted a big family, and he was a smidge jealous of Stefan who already was a father of three. "Until you agree, I'm happy spending my days spoiling you and our little harvest blessing."

About the Liza Kay

Liza grew up in a tiny village in Germany, the kind where you know everybody and everybody knows you. She migrated to a bigger town to attend college, although her parents often wonder if she really moved out. Now, with a degree in her pocket, she's perfectly capable of working as a librarian. Never one to do what's expected of her, Liza currently browses different branches of employment.

She started writing in college when she found herself unable to ignore the guys living in her head any longer, and to distract herself from the stifling, non-fiction stuff taught in class. Liza is really fond of the dudes whispering in her mind—no matter if handsome or flawed, big or small, sulky or easy-going. They all deserve love and their HEAs.

When she's not writing, you can find her curled up with a good book and a cup of tea, a cat in her lap, or a camera at the ready.

You can contact her at onelizakay@gmail.com
Or visit her blog at https://onelizakay.wordpress.com/

QUINTESSENCE

BY

SUEDE DELRAY

Hamish and Liam are looking for peace, but two immortal beings have other plans.

After a traumatic experience in Yemen, Liam is tormented by bad memories. The couple come to settle in a small New England town, where Hamish believes Liam can heal. When strange things begin happening and two unexpected guests arrive, their plans are thrown to the Autumn wind. An Angel and a demon, with a history of their own, are in battle for Hamish's soul, and with each other.

CHAPTER ONE: HAMISH

The scars Liam had inside were far harder to heal than the ones he'd had on his face. Although Hamish had covertly healed the scars on Liam's face before he even knew they were there, he felt quite helpless when it came to the psychological trauma his lover was experiencing.

As Hamish watched Liam unpacking some of the boxes that had just arrived, he thought about erasing the memory of what Liam had witnessed in Yemen, but that would be wrong. What had happened was part of Liam now, and it wasn't right to steal his memories, even if they were fraught with pain.

Liam's symptoms had begun shortly after he'd witnessed a bomb attack by Saudi Arabian forces on a school bus in Sanaa. "Fifty-one people are dead," Liam had told Hamish, tears running down his face. "Forty of them are children. Children, Hamish."

Perhaps the attack on the school bus had been the straw that broke the camel's back, as they said. The armed conflict between the Yemeni government and the Houthi had taken its toll. Women and children were dying every day, if not by war then by the widespread cholera outbreak.

Doctors without Borders had been Liam's passion. Yes, he'd lost some, but the ones he'd saved had filled his life with meaning. Hamish stayed by his side, acting as interpreter and providing moral support. They hadn't needed any encounters with supernatural evil in Yemen. Evil was all around them.

After the bus explosion, Liam would wake up in the

middle of the night. He'd walk the floor. He had nightmares. "There's no reason to go on," he told Hamish one night. "Violence and hate are endless, Hamish. What's the point of the world? What was the point of you sealing the portal?"

It had taken months for Hamish to convince Liam that they needed to leave Yemen, start over somewhere else, where the sounds of death and gunfire didn't constantly ring out in the night. It wasn't easy for either of them. They were leaving helpless people who needed them, people who had no choice but to stay.

Hamish began to look for a quiet town where Liam could heal. Thankfully, one of the other doctors working in the program had told them about a place in Vermont. "The family doctor there is my uncle. He's retiring," she'd said. "He wants to sell his house and move to Miami, but he won't leave until another doctor is found."

"What's this place like?" Hamish had asked.

"Ski resort, very quiet. Nearest city is Rutland, only a twenty-minute drive."

It was Liam who came to understand that Hamish was right about needing to leave. One night during an emergency, he froze. A child was brought in, no more than three, with a badly damaged leg caused by a stray bullet. There was a lot of blood. When Liam saw the blood and realized that part of the leg was gone, he had a flashback of the bus attack. It paralyzed him. "I couldn't move," he told Hamish. "Thankfully, Doctor Boisvert was there with me. You're right. I need to leave."

"Look what I found," Liam said, suddenly bringing Hamish's thoughts back to the present.

Hamish focused on the figure of the male angel he'd bought years ago in New York City. "Wow," he said, taking it from Liam. "It survived."

"So have we," Liam said, hugging Hamish's arm briefly

before moving away. "But you're going to be in trouble if you don't help me unpack these boxes, lazybones."

Hamish grinned as he started to take the tape off a large carton. "You never did tell me what you thought of the place?"

"The house or the town?" Liam queried.

"Both, I guess." Hamish waited. Liam had put up no resistance when Hamish told him about Killington, a town in the Green Mountains with a population of no more than nine hundred. On the other hand, he hadn't exactly jumped up and down when they'd arrived at the rustic cottage surrounded by the Green Mountains and the Gifford Woods State Park.

"I love the house," Liam said, looking around. It was like a cabin, everything wood, with open spaces and a fireplace. Out their window they could see beautiful sugar maples, whose leaves were now changing to vivid shades of red and orange. There were no neighbors for a mile or two, just trees and grass, and breathtaking mountains.

Hamish waited. "And the town?"

"It's a tourist place." He looked at Hamish. "A place to ski, which I don't."

"We could learn how." Hamish met his gaze.

"Yes, you're right, and Rutland is close by," Liam said absently. "The clinic is okay, I guess. I met the nurse, Monica Prue, yesterday. She's had twenty years of experience, which is good so she can show me the ropes. She told me that it was quiet, which is what I need. Family medicine and an occasional skiing accident should keep the ghosts at bay."

Hamish put a hand on his shoulder. "It's not forever. I know you're used to working in a big hospital or with the Borders' program. Maybe you'll learn to appreciate the quiet life for a while."

Liam smiled. "My eternal optimist. I'm going to do my best to make this work, Hamish. I promise. If you are by my side,

I'll do okay."

Hamish took Liam into his arms and held him close. "I want you to be well, baby."

"I will be," he said, kissing Hamish quickly on the mouth. "Now let's get this place in order."

With half the boxes unpacked, they took a break. Hamish made pasta for dinner, and they shared a little wine. With the medication Liam had been prescribed for anxiety, he only drank half a glass.

They sat in front of the fireplace, watching the embers dancing. Liam fell asleep with his head in Hamish's lap. After a while, Hamish lifted Liam's head and stood up. Retrieving a spare blanket from the bedroom, he covered him and put a pillow under his head. Anytime Liam was peacefully asleep was good. Even with the medication, he still wasn't sleeping well.

Hamish walked outside, quietly closing the door behind him. It was cold tonight, but Hamish didn't mind the temperature change. He didn't feel the elements like mortals did. He sat down on the stoop and looked up at the night sky. It was so clear — the stars bright and the moon three-quarters full. It was ironic how powerful time was. As it moved, changes happened faster than anyone could anticipate.

It seemed only moments ago he'd been given the sword of Gideon that he'd used to send the demons back to hell. Frank, an angel, had helped him, perishing in the fight. But four years had gone by since Hamish's hybrid status of angel-demon was needed to save the world. Unfortunately, evil could never be kept at bay. You pushed it down, and it found a way to rise again.

When Hamish's wings had changed completely to white, shedding all specks of black, he took it in stride — a message that all was good. Then his wings had turned inward, staying there, resting maybe. His entire universe became Liam, his best friend, his lover. In this place, he wasn't sure what he would do when Liam was working at the clinic. Maybe farming, growing things, maple syrup. There were endless possibilities when he wasn't saving the world.

The wind kicked up now, battering the beauty of new autumn foliage on the trees. Soon the leaves would fall to the ground, providing a majestic carpet awaiting the coming snow. Far away, above the whooshing of the wind, he could hear the wolves, moose, and black bears. They roamed the mountains and the woods, all in search of their prey.

As Hamish prepared to go inside, he paused. Something began to gnaw at him. It was almost an itch he felt compelled to scratch but couldn't locate. It started deep in his gut and rose to his throat, then radiated around to his back. As soon as it came, it was gone. Hamish breathed a sigh of relief. It was nothing but a distant echo.

He went back inside and locked the door. He checked on Liam, still sleeping, and bent to kiss him. He crawled into bed alone, closed his eyes, and tried to sleep. Outside, he could hear the whispering of the wind. *Hamish.*

Chapter Two: Liam

Liam was standing at the counter, making coffee when Hamish came out of the bedroom. "Hey," Hamish said, coming over to kiss him. "Coffee ready?"

"Just about," Liam said. "Did you sleep okay?"

"You know me," Hamish said. "I sleep or I don't, doesn't affect me much. And you?"

He shrugged. If one called waking up periodically in a cold sweat *sleeping*.

"At least you don't sleep standing up anymore."

Liam laughed. When he'd first met Hamish, he'd been on a mission from the Dark Lord to bring Liam to the underworld. Hamish had fallen in love with him and saved him. "That was creepy when I saw you sleep standing up in the corner."

"I wasn't really sleeping," Hamish said. "I prefer to sleep beside you now."

Liam looked over at him. Hamish was so beautiful. He was the sexiest man he'd ever seen and a great lover. Since Yemen, however, their sex life had been practically nonexistent. The anxiety meds didn't help. It wasn't because he didn't want to. In his head, he imagined Hamish touching him, holding him, but the erection just didn't come, and if it did, he couldn't hold on to it long enough.

Hamish told him he understood, that he'd be patient. "You've been through a lot, baby. You won't need to take those pills forever."

"What if I do? What if we can never have sex again,

Hamish?"

Liam handed Hamish a cup of coffee now, and they sat together at the kitchen counter, sipping the brew quietly.

"I'm going in to the clinic today," Liam announced. "Thought I'd take a look at the patient files. You don't mind?" It was time. He'd start seeing patients in two days.

"No. I'll finish the unpacking," Hamish told him. "Do you want to go to dinner tonight? There is a nice restaurant in the village."

"Sounds good," Liam said. "What are you going to do here to occupy your time, Hamish?"

"I don't know yet. I was thinking about growing food."

Liam laughed. "Okay. A country farmer?"

"Something like that. I'll figure it out. I don't want you to worry about it. Did you take your pills?"

"Yes, sir," Liam told him, saluting. He hated them, but they took the edge off. He got up and rinsed his cup in the sink. "If you need the vehicle, you'll have to drive me to town and pick me up later."

"I'd pick you up anytime." Hamish smirked.

"Flirt," Liam accused. He gazed over at him. "God, I love you so much." That was true. He walked over and kissed him deeply.

"That was promising," Hamish said, releasing him.

"Delicious." Liam grinned and headed to the bedroom.

"I'll drive you in case I need the vehicle," Hamish said, following him down the hallway. "We might want to get another vehicle?"

"Good idea," Liam said.

"Did you eat?"

"I ate a muffin. I left you one."

"What about lunch?" Hamish asked as Liam was gathering together his keys and wallet.

"I don't know yet."

"I'll bring you lunch," Hamish told him, taking off his robe.

Liam paused to admire the view. Hamish had a beautiful body. He wanted to touch him, kiss his broad shoulders, nibble the round, hard cheeks of his ass. When Hamish turned around, Liam's eyes widened. The scars where his wings exited looked different. "Ah, Hamish?"

Hamish glanced at him over his shoulder. "Yeah, baby?"

Liam swallowed and came closer. He ran a finger over one of the red, ragged slashes. As he did, he pushed with his finger and thumb. It was opening. There was no blood, no sign of feathers yet, but when he lay his hand over the gash, there was a faint vibration.

"What is it?" Hamish sounded panicky. "What's wrong? Let me see?" He was trying to turn around, look in the mirror.

Liam stood back to let him see. Hamish ran into the bathroom, got a hand mirror, came back out and studied his back in the long mirror on the bedroom wall. He put the mirror down.

"It could be nothing," Liam said, chewing his bottom lip.

"It's how it begins." Hamish sighed. He put down the mirror. "But why now? Why here?"

Liam had no answer. All he could say is, "Let's not worry until we need to."

"Okay," Hamish said, but didn't look convinced. "I'll just finish dressing and drive you to town."

"Thanks. I'll warm up the SUV." Liam shrugged into his jacket and walked out onto the porch. He breathed in some fresh mountain air and unlocked the vehicle. He glanced up at the big maple tree, admiring its colors. He watched the leaves gently fall to the ground. Something didn't quite seem right. There was a pile of leaves at least four feet high all around the circumference of the tree trunk, yet the tree was still in full foliage. That was strange.

When Hamish came outside, Liam pointed to the tree.

"How did all those leaves end up over there you think?"

Hamish shrugged, not appearing to be too interested. "I don't know. Maybe the direction of the wind."

Liam knew he had other things on his mind. "Is your back sore?" Liam asked him, changing the subject.

Hamish started the engine. "No. But last night I felt itchy. It was weird. It didn't last, so I figured it for a fluke."

Liam fell silent. Every time Hamish's wings appeared, it meant something was up. But what could possibly be wrong out here in the middle of nowhere?

Hamish dropped him off at the clinic but didn't stay. He said something about needing to go home and finish unpacking.

Liam stood on the street corner and watched him go. He was worried.

The clinic was on the ground floor of a two-story building. On the second floor there was a small infirmary, and right beside him was the drug store.

He keyed opened the door and walked in. The waiting room was impeccable. There was a big desk in front for the secretary. He hadn't met her yet. The nurse's office was to the left, and at the end of the hallway was the doctor's office and examining rooms. The name *Doctor Samuel Morgan* was still on the door.

Liam walked in and fired up the computer. The password was taped to the desk. He'd change it once he got into the files. As he began to read the patient profiles, he forgot about everything.

When he heard a familiar voice calling to him, he sat back in his swivel chair and rubbed his eyes. "In here, Hamish," he called out. "What time is it?"

Hamish walked in with a picnic hamper. "It's lunchtime."

Liam laughed. "I've lost all sense of time, it seems. What's with the picnic basket? Are we eating outside?"

"Ha, ha. I couldn't find anything else to put it in. I made tuna sandwiches, and there's potato salad." He began unpacking the food.

"Yum." Liam grinned. "You made the potato salad?"

"Right," he said, making a face as he put down paper plates. "The supermarket made it, or some company from" — he eyed the label—"New York."

"That's okay. I'm hungry," Liam said, taking a bite of his sandwich. He checked the clock. "It's almost one o'clock." He eyed him. "Are you okay?"

Hamish sat back in a chair across from Liam and forked potato salad into his mouth. "I guess. We'll be all right here." He grabbed a sandwich. "Is there coffee?"

"Yes, there's one of those coffee pod machines in the kitchen. Want some?"

"Later. So, interesting patient files?" Hamish asked as they ate.

"Usual—diabetes, problems with blood pressure, arthritis, repetitive strain injury, heart attacks, nothing to write home about." He took some more of the potato salad. "This is good, probably not good for you, but tasty."

Hamish smiled. "Are you hanging around, or would you like me to come back?"

"I have other things to do," Liam said. "There are some prescriptions to renew that are close to expiring. I should do that right away and give them to the pharmacist. It'll save me time next week."

"Okay."

"Have a coffee first," Liam said, once again glancing at the screen.

"No, I'll leave you to it, take this home. Call me when you're finished. I'll come and get you."

Liam got to his feet, kissed him. "Thanks, gorgeous."

After Hamish left, Liam concentrated on his patient files again, deciding which prescriptions he needed to renew right away, and which could wait.

When he heard a noise out in the waiting area, Liam thought Hamish had come back again. Liam hadn't bothered locking the door behind him. Maybe he should have. "Hamish, did you forget something?"

A young man was standing in the reception area—a stranger. Blond with light azure blue eyes, he was boyish with a slight frame and a sublime smile. "Hello, Liam," he said softly. His voice was fine and a little higher pitched than one would expect from a young man of say, twenty.

"Ah, hello." Liam raised an eyebrow. "Do I know you?" He'd called him Liam. His name wasn't even on the door yet.

"No," he said, "but I know you." He looked around. "I must have missed Hamish. Do you know where he is now?"

"Hamish? What do you want with Hamish?" Liam folded his arms across his chest.

"Oh, much, but not to be worried." He looked around. "Have you been visited by anyone else?"

"We just moved here. We don't know anyone. And I don't know you, so I suggest you leave now."

He seemed unphased by Liam's demand. "I mean him no harm. It's only his soul I'm after."

Liam swallowed hard. "His . . . ah . . . soul?"

"Yes, I am in a battle with someone. I will not say his name." Those iridescent eyes glowed. "I will leave you. Please, tell Hamish that I will visit him soon."

"Who or what are you?" Liam demanded.

"Tell him that Azrael is here. Hamish will understand." He turned and left without so much as a goodbye.

Liam sank into one of the chairs in the waiting room. It took him a few minutes before he could pick up the phone and call

Hamish.

Hamish answered on the second ring. "Liam? You want to come home now?"

"Yes, but that's not what I'm calling for. I had a visitor. Who's Azrael?"

"Azrael?" Hamish echoed.

"He said he wanted to see you. Hamish, he wasn't human. And he said he was in a battle with someone for your soul. He didn't want to say the name. Who's Azrael, and what in the hell is this about?"

"Nothing to do with hell. Azrael is an archangel."

"Oh shit." Liam sat again, running a hand through his hair. "What does he want with you, and who's he fighting with?"

"I don't know. I guess we'll find out soon enough. Get ready. I'll be there in ten minutes."

"Okay."

On the way back home, Hamish took Liam's hand. "He didn't hurt you?"

"No. He's like that angel you brought at Christmas time in New York. He's so soft-spoken, blond and blue-eyed, almost androgynous. Do you think this has something to do with what we noticed this morning with your back?"

"It could, I suppose."

As they pulled up onto the road leading to their house, Liam gasped. He pointed to the house. "What in the world is going on?" The pile of leaves under the tree had gotten higher. They were beginning to spread out, expanding like a woven path around one side of the house.

Hamish put on the brakes and then slammed the vehicle into park. "What in the name of —" He jumped out of the vehicle.

Liam scrambled out after him. They stood looking in awe at the tapestry of brightly colored leaves.

Then the front door opened. A figure stood there, tall, broad-shouldered with jet-black hair. He was dressed in black with a long coat flapping around his knee-high boots.

"What are you doing here?" Hamish demanded.

When he walked to the edge of the porch, Liam couldn't deny how beautiful he was. There was a strong masculine sexuality that embodied him like a shroud. He smiled, and Liam felt weak.

Hamish placed a hand on Liam to hold him up. "What do you want, Ravish?"

As the one Hamish called Ravish descended the steps, Liam felt his heartbeat quicken. Ravish looked deeply into Liam's eyes. "I can take away your pain."

Liam felt himself falling, and darkness claimed him.

CHAPTER THREE: RAVISH

R avish realized that Hamish was seriously peeved at him. "Not angry enough to smite me with that angel sword you got hidden away, are you?" Ravish eyed him with a smirk.

Hamish narrowed his eyes. "Maybe."

Ravish followed him into the bedroom, watching the way Hamish lovingly put Liam on the bed.

Hamish gave him a shove out of the room and closed the bedroom door. He stood glaring at him like an angry bull. "You leave Liam alone. You know the effect you have on mortals."

"I didn't do anything to your lover-boy," Ravish told him, walking around the living room, picking up this and that. He spotted the male angel and held it up in the light. "Looks like that impotent little snot, Azrael. Didn't know he was marketing his own image now. Wonder if you can buy them on eBay."

"Put that down." Hamish took it from him. "Don't touch anything. What's going on, Ravish? What are you and that archangel doing here?"

"Skiing?" Ravish suggested then chuckled.

"Funny. Try again."

"We're certainly not here together, if that's what you mean. He's arrogant and rather stupid. He did this." Ravish floated his hand around the room. "With the leaves," he added when Hamish didn't seem to know what he was talking about. "He's trying to trap me here. Now he's trapped us all. I don't think he knows how to undo this, either. The leaves are just going to keep on winding around and around." He threw himself on the sofa.

"That's ridiculous," Hamish said. "He can't do that. Mortals will see it."

"I don't think he's concerned by that. He learned this trick from some sorcerer back in the bad old days. I've seen him do it with snow, too. Impressive, I must say. Those angels, they don't know what side they're on though. You can't be good all the time, can you?" Ravish looked at Hamish for an answer.

"I don't give a damn about any of that. You still didn't tell me what you're doing in my house."

"You already know, Hamish. Azrael and I are in competition for your soul. White feathers, dark feathers, in between feathers. We need you to pick a side, even if it's rather arbitrary."

"Even mortals aren't all good or bad, how can they expect us to be?" Hamish sighed. "What if I decide not to?"

Ravish was thinking about that. He had a point.

"Anyway, it kind of chooses me. I don't have control. Who sent you, the Dark Lord?" Hamish asked.

"None of that matters, Hamish. Just commit your soul to me, and I'll be gone."

"You're not going anywhere," a soft voice announced.

Ravish and Hamish looked around to see Azrael standing in the doorway.

Ravish rolled his eyes. "Undo the spell, angel boy. You know I'm going to win this time."

Azrael looked at Hamish. "You've already earned your place with us, my friend. He has no claim on your soul."

Ravish regarded the angel with half-closed eyes. Damn. If only that irritable little cherub didn't stiffen his cock every time he laid eyes on him.

Ravish rose up to his full height. The blond-haired imp could try and hide his desire for him all he wanted, but Ravish could smell it on him. "Isn't lust one of the deadly sins?" he asked seductively.

"Only if it's your neighbor's wife, I believe," he replied, smiling.

Ravish shook his head. "Crazy rules, you Goodies have. Too bad, because right now, I'm undressing you in my head and you couldn't imagine what delights I could bestow. But then" — he sniffed — "I'm not interested in your skinny angel ass."

"Well, then I suggest you get those images of my naked body out of your head, demon boy. It's never going to happen again. Keep your filthy thoughts and paws to yourself."

"What's going on here?" Hamish demanded, looking from one to another, his eyes wide. "Are you two . . . ah . . . into each other?"

"I'm not into him," Azrael denied, withdrawing his sword. "I am here to do battle for your soul, and if I have to draw and quarter this sleazy pervert to do it, I will."

"Sleazy pervert, eh?" Ravish moved up closer. "Who almost lost their wings due to lack of control? I was thrown to the wolves because of you. Who walked away without so much as a tap on the wrist?"

"You seduced me," Azrael accused. "And it's not my fault your tribunal is less forgiving than mine."

"You chained me to a wall and had your way with me!" Ravish accused. He had rather enjoyed that, but still, there were consequences. "You act all innocent, but you are as much of a pervert as I am."

Azrael moved forward. "I was doing my job, slaying demons."

"Yes, but you didn't slay me, did you? Instead, you —"

"Whoa!" Hamish shouted, moving in between them.

"Listen, this is getting out of control. Kill each other or fuck each other, I don't care what you decide, but do it somewhere else." Hamish pointed at the angel. "Get rid of those leaves around my house."

He put his sword back into its sheaf and pointed at Ravish. "He worked the spell, not I. Ask him."

"Lying is also a sin," Ravish challenged. Damn, but he was cute when he got angry.

"Angels don't lie."

"Ha!" Ravish scoffed. "Should I give you a list?"

"Someone did it," Hamish protested. "So undo it. And be forewarned, it doesn't matter who wins or loses here, I will choose what to do with my soul, and you can tell whoever sent you, I said so. Now, go away, both of you."

Ravish walked to the door and opened it. He pointed outside. "Ah, doesn't look like we're going anywhere until this is settled." He pointed to the ceiling. "Higher power."

Hamish's eyes widened as he looked outside. In the distance, the leaves had formed a barrier around the property as high as a ten-foot fence. "Damn it," Hamish said. "This is completely insane."

"You said it," Ravish grunted. "Stuck here with Goodie-Two-Shoes when I could be having fun being worshipped and adored by an array of juicy mortal morsels."

"And me, stuck with Mr. Personality," Azrael said, shaking his head. "And what juicy mortal morsels?"

Ravish laughed. "Jealous much?"

"Oh, for the love of—" Hamish threw up his hands. "Get a room, you two. I'm going to see if Liam is all right." He pointed at them. "Try not to shed blood while I'm gone."

Ravish watched him go. "Alone at last, Angel Cake. Let's talk this out. You want his soul. I want his soul. You want to get away from me, and I want the same. We both know you tried to trap me here. So, remove the spell."

"It wasn't me."

"Well, it sure as heaven wasn't me. You just don't want to admit that you can't get enough of me."

"I'll show you enough, you devilish fiend." Azrael raised a hand and sent Ravish flying up to the ceiling.

Ravish hit the ceiling hard, laughing. "This is fun!" Ravish dropped down to the floor, landing on his feet. "That all you got, girlie boy?"

Azrael let out a shout and charged him. They struggled in mid-air. Ravish pulled him closer. "I could kiss you at this moment, Angel."

Azrael stuck the point of his sword to the top of Ravish's groin. "And I could incapacitate you, demon, permanently."

"That wouldn't be nice," Ravish whispered, licking Azrael's face slowly with his tongue. "You'd be sorry. I wouldn't be much use to you."

Azrael tried to get away from him, but Ravish held him firm. "Your power is waning," he said softly in his ear. "You want me. Desire is weakening you. Do you remember what it felt like when I was inside you, Azrael?"

Azrael's body went limp. His sword languished at his side. He looked into Ravish's eyes. "You don't play fair," he said softly. "You never did."

"I'm a demon. We don't know fair," he told him. "Kiss me. And I promise we will work out a solution to the problem, preferably in bed."

Ravish's mouth moved closer to his. He could almost taste his angel kisses, but just as their mouths met, the sword came up again, this time against his side. "Let me go, or I'll gut you," Azrael threatened.

Their gazes met, locked. "I'd die for a kiss from you." Ravish grabbed Azrael's blond hair and pulled back his head, smothering his mouth with his. Then Ravish pushed the angel away and flew around the room, landing on the other side of it.

Azrael made a big deal of wiping the kiss off his mouth. "There is no working out a compromise with you, demon. Hamish will choose, or we will battle it out."

"They have bigger problems," Ravish said, taking a seat on the sofa.

"What problems?"

"No sex," he whispered.

"That has nothing to do with us. What are we now, marriage counselors?"

"Liam is traumatized. He was in Yemen. I saw the scenes of horror in his head."

"Another place where your evil reigns."

"I don't do evil." Ravish objected. "I punish evildoers. I collect the souls from your side." He smiled. "Mortals commit far more atrocities than I can ever dream up."

"Why would you want to help Liam, anyway?" Azrael leaned against the mantle.

"Hamish will be grateful, pledge his allegiance to the dark side. Then I can stay."

"Stay? Among the mortals?" Azrael asked him.

"Yes. I don't fit anywhere. I get tired of doing the same thing all the time." Ravish looked over at him, his voice softening. "I only competed for this job because I knew I'd see you again."

"More of your bullshit. You wanted to see me to get revenge for something you did."

Azrael had said it, but Ravish noticed he looked away when he did.

"Anyway, that was a long time ago. We have other matters to contend with. I can heal Liam too. I am the angel that can heal emotional scars, anxiety."

"But you won't. Just like Hamish won't."

"Because taking away that pain will take his memories too,

and that's part of him," Azrael said almost to himself. "It's always a tradeoff, but I could just get rid of the effects, leave the memory."

"You softie, you." Ravish teased. "I do admit you have the advantage over me there. However, it doesn't mean it's enough to win Hamish's soul."

Azrael rolled his eyes. "So, we are back to square one."

"Apparently," Ravish replied, smiling.

Chapter Four: Hamish

"Who in the world are they?" Liam asked. "And what are they doing in our living room?"

"Just calm down, Liam. It will be all right. I know them."

"That doesn't make me feel any better, Hamish. You know the Dark Lord too, and I wouldn't want to see him in our living room. What do they want? Who was that guy that made me pass out, and why are there two of them now?"

"That was Ravish on the porch. He has a powerful effect on mortals who —" Hamish didn't really want to tell him the rest.

"Who what? Why did I faint?"

"Ravish has a lot of sexual allure. Mortals in need of sexual attention often fall victim to him a little faster." Hamish winced.

"Oh, great." Liam threw up his hands. "Now it's confirmed. I've become an asexual, impotent loser."

Hamish sat beside him and stroked his hair. "Sweetie, that's not true. You've been through a lot. It takes times to come back to what you were, that's all. We had a wonderful sex life, and I'm sure that —"

"Had. That's the operative word. Maybe it would have been better if I'd never gone to Yemen."

"How can you say that? You did wonderful things there. You want to forget the wonderful people you met and saved?" Hamish met his gaze.

"No," Liam said. "But I want to be with you again, make love to you the way I used to, hear you call out my name. I know you miss me. I miss you too. These damn pills, they make me—"

"I know baby," Hamish said. "We'll find a solution. But for the time being, we have to decide what to do about those guys." He hooked a thumb toward the door.

"So one is a sex demon named Ravish, and the other, that blond guy from the office, he's a"—Liam paused—"an angel."

Hamish nodded.

"They're here for your soul." Liam took his hand. "What are we going to do?"

"No one can take my soul. They can battle all they want, but I will be the one to decide."

"Do you have to decide at all?" Liam clutched his arm.

"I'm really not sure yet. Anyway, the good news is they don't seem to be totally focused on my soul." He grinned.

"What do you mean?" Liam asked.

"Well, it's the weirdest thing, but I think they may be ah . . . in love."

"In love with who?" Liam asked.

"Each other." Hamish looked toward the door.

"What? Is that possible, an angel and a demon?" Liam's eyes widened.

"Permitted? No. Possible, yes. Azrael and Ravish have met before."

"You know them, don't you, and not just by reputation?"

Hamish nodded.

"Okay." Liam came a little closer. "Fess up, boy. How do you know them?"

"Well, a zillion years ago, Archangels were dispatched to cull the herd of demons, so to speak."

"That's terrible," Liam exclaimed. "A demon genocide."

Hamish nodded. "I guess."

"Why?"

"Demons were beginning to outnumber the angels, and there was concern that the world would be unbalanced."

"So, where did you figure into all this?"

"I was the lord of the Place In Between. I couldn't take sides in the dispute, although the dark Lord insisted that I provide a haven for demons on the run."

"And you defied him," Liam said.

Hamish grinned. "You know me well. But I didn't exactly defy him."

Liam waited.

"Instead, I made a decision to be Switzerland."

Liam took his hand. "You offered help to both sides."

He shrugged.

"You devilish angel," Liam teased him. "So, that's when you met them?"

"I already knew Ravish. He had a big reputation. Sometimes I'd find him roaming the streets of the Place In Between."

"He was a kindred spirit," Liam concluded. "He, too, wanted to escape what he was."

"Yes, but he was far too important, and the Dark Lord kept him on a tight leash."

"When did Azrael come into the story?" Liam enquired. "Were he and Ravish lovers?"

Hamish kissed Liam on the top of the head. "My little romantic. I don't know the entire story. They met, they battled. Azrael combed The Place in Between looking for Ravish. That's all I know. But when I see them together now, I sense their history is complicated. It seems like a mix of lust combined with dislike and a really fatal attraction."

"If we can get them together," Liam insisted, "maybe they'll forget about fighting over your soul and ride off into the sunset."

"You aren't seriously suggesting we play matchmaker for

a demon and an angel?" Hamish was smiling.

"Why not?" Liam asked. "We're not exactly your typical couple, are we?"

"No, but it's forbidden."

Liam reached up and stroked Hamish's hair. "And when has that stopped you, my rebellious darling?"

Hamish thought about it for a minute. It could work. "Okay, I'm in, if it means we can get rid of them."

"Good." Liam walked over to the window. "Ah, Hamish?" He looked over his shoulder. "Why is there a fence made of . . . are those leaves all around our house?"

Hamish came over and put his arm around him. "There are a lot of trees in Vermont."

Liam looked up at him, made a face. "Seriously?"

"Come on, my little matchmaker, let's get out there and see if there's any blood that needs mopping up."

"Blood? What blood?" Liam hurried out of the bedroom, practically on the back of Hamish's heels.

The first thing Hamish noticed when he got to the living room was Ravish standing in the corner. He was sleeping.

Azrael was sitting on the chair in front of the fire, reading a novel Hamish had just started.

Liam walked over to Ravish and examined him. His eyes were open, but he was definitely asleep.

"Creepy, isn't it?" Azrael said, putting aside the novel. "I sleep standing too, but at least I close my eyes."

"Hamish used to do that," Liam told him. "He sleeps in bed with me now."

"Love." Azrael sighed. "If I had a reason, maybe I'd try the bed too."

"I'm sure Ravish would sleep beside you if you asked him," Hamish suggested.

"Why in creation would I want that mangy demon sleeping with me?" Azrael shook his head.

133

"What happened between you two?" Liam asked. "Were you once a couple?"

"A couple, with him? No. He's a demon, Liam. I'm an angel. That wouldn't be permitted." Azrael stuck his nose in the air.

"Maybe not," Hamish said, sitting on the sofa. "But something happened, didn't it, that time when you were hunting him in The Place in Between?"

"Long time ago, ancient history. Subject change," Azrael announced. "Since he's asleep, listen to me." He looked at Hamish. "You saved the world from a demon invasion. You're in. Our side has claimed you, Hamish."

"Makes him sound like the movie of the week," Liam chuckled. "Superhero saves the world and earns his wings."

Hamish found that funny. He laughed. "White ones, don't forget."

"Of course, baby," Liam replied. "But I was kind of partial to the ones with black flecks."

"Naughty boy." Hamish blew him a kiss.

Azrael frowned. "Listen, seriously. Hamish, you don't want your soul going to the dark lord, do you?"

"The dark lord and I are no longer on speaking terms," Hamish said. "But I don't want to give my soul away without knowing the conditions."

"Conditions?" Azrael echoed.

"Yes, conditions, Angel Boy," another voice rang out. "Nothing is without conditions."

They all looked over at Ravish, now wide awake.

"Don't listen to him, Hamish," Azrael protested. "Liam, please make Hamish see reason. You are a good, God-fearing mortal man. You don't want Hamish's soul rotting in hell, do you?"

"Hamish will make up his own mind, Azrael," Liam told him. "And it's my experience that nothing is at all like I learned in Sunday school."

Ravish clapped his hands as he came forward. "Bravo, Liam. You are correct. These outdated stories of heaven and hell don't fly anymore. I can't believe you would stoop so low, Azrael, to use the old fire and brimstone rhetoric to scare our friends here."

"Some of us hold to tradition," Azrael retorted.

"Traditions with no basis in reality?" Ravish told him. "Redundant, no?"

Azrael ignored that.

Ravish turned to Liam. "Don't think that Azrael's offer comes without stipulations. And I apologize for before. It was rude of me to invade your thoughts on our first meeting, Liam. It's rather a habit of mine."

"Apology accepted, on one condition," Liam said.

"That being?" Ravish smiled at him.

Hamish shot him a dirty look. "Tone it down."

"Sorry," he said. "What is it you want, Liam?"

"You tell us the story of your first meeting with Azrael," Liam explained.

"It would be my pleasure." Ravish bowed his head.

Azrael exploded with anger. "You would ask him, a demon, and not me, who is the epitome of truth and purity, to tell you our history?"

Ravish began to laugh.

"And what are you laughing at, demon?" Azrael glared at him.

"Just funny to watch you get so angry. Angels are supposed to be so good-natured."

They moved toward each other, threateningly.

"Ah, ah." Hamish jumped up and pushed them apart. "We are eager to hear both sides of the story."

Ravish sat down in a chair. He leaned back, arms across his chest. "You can even go first, Angel Cakes. Then after you finish, I'll tell them what really happened."

Azrael grumbled under his breath. "We are wasting time. We need to decide this contest and take our leave." He looked at Hamish. "This is about your soul, not about Ravish and me."

Hamish put up a hand. "I need to show you both something." He stood up and began to undo his shirt.

"Can't wait." Ravish made a sound of pleasure in his throat, licking his lips. "Should we put on some music?"

"Only the shirt, demon. Calm yourself." Hamish turned around to show his back.

Ravish and Azrael approached, both marveling over the openings in Hamish's shoulder blades.

"There are no feathers yet," Hamish informed them. "But it's only a matter of time. Nothing can be decided until the feathers start to emerge." He turned to them. "The decision will be made for us."

Ravish looked at him. "Unless your wings return to their original color, a mix of white and black. It will then be time to decide or fight." Ravish looked at Azrael. "We may have to battle after all."

"I look forward to running you through with my sword," Azrael told him.

Ravish threw his dark head back and laughed.

"So, in the meantime" — Hamish put his shirt back on — "we wait."

"Yes," Liam chimed in. "So, we have time for a story. Azrael, you go first. Ravish, you mustn't interrupt him until he's finished. You'll have your turn later. Agreed?"

Ravish retook his seat. He looked at Azrael. "You have the floor, my angelic friend. Try not to put me to sleep."

Chapter Five: Azrael

Time didn't have the same meaning to angelic beings. It all just seemed to seamlessly drift from century to century. Azrael's existence was uncomplicated. He knew his role—to heal the distressed and escort the dying to another plain. That was all he knew.

When Michael, the great warrior, protector of all that was good in the world, told them they were at war, everything had changed. Azrael's contact with demons was minimal, to say the least. They were there because they had to be, to balance the world order, and Azrael rarely gave them a thought. In the Between was Hamish, the hybrid, who stood as the fork in the road, the great tour guide, someone else Azrael had no reason to associate with.

"Demons are multiplying," Michael had told them. "A devious plan by the Dark Lord to unbalance the universe. We are at war. Your mission is to hunt demons and destroy as many as you can. Go."

That was it. Each with their sword, they took different paths and fought the good fight. Azrael had no idea how many of his demon adversaries he had cut down, but by the time he came face to face with the one they called Ravish, he was dog tired. More than that, he felt quite sad and alone. Killing one demon after another had demoralized him.

Ravish appeared when he was most vulnerable.

He'd been warned about Ravish. "He is a trickster," Uriel, one of the other archangels told Azrael. "And he doesn't seem entirely committed to the dark side, either. They say he's a rebel, often found wandering the Place in Between. Like Hamish, he's a malcontent. He is a great seducer."

"He will not seduce me," Azrael boasted.

"I've sensed your loneliness, my brother," Uriel confessed. "Ravish is beautiful, a robustly sexual demon without loyalty to any cause. If you should encounter him, be on your guard."

Uriel wasn't kidding. The first time Azrael confronted Ravish, it was at an Inn, where every mortal appeared to be intoxicated and sexually aroused. And most of them hadn't even been drinking.

"Have you succeeded in having sexual relations with every patron, Ravish?" Azrael called out to him. He found him out behind the Inn.

The moon was glowing overhead, the stars bright in the sky that night. He watched Ravish smack the mortal on the ass. "Go now, inside," he urged. "Do up your breeches."

Azrael waited for the mortal man to scurry past then moved closer to Ravish. He withdrew his sword.

"Azrael," Ravish said, clapping his hands, "I was wondering when we'd meet. Your reputation proceeds you."

"Really? So does yours, and from what I've just witnessed, it's well deserved." Azrael ran his gaze over him. Yes, Ravish was beautiful, divinely so, with thick, black hair and illuminating dark eyes. His face was truly a thing of beauty, with sensuous lips and high cheekbones. And he was tall, with a lithe, muscular body.

"Thank you so much," Ravish said. "You're not bad yourself, in a very feminine sort of way."

"Don't read my thoughts. It's rude." Azrael glared at him.

"A talent of mine. I'm sorry. I can't resist. Your thoughts are so intriguing. Are you female, male, or something in between?" Ravish peered at him. "Whatever it is, it's very stimulating."

Azrael moved forward. "Enough. Prepare to fight," Azrael

lunged at him. When he did, he found nothing but air. He turned. Ravish was sitting on top of the Inn's thatched roof. He waved at him.

Azrael flew up in the air and grabbed the demon by the throat. He knocked him off the roof, propelling him toward a tree, where he pinned him. Ravish was laughing at him, which made Azrael angry. They were so close, Azrael could feel his body melding against his. His powers grew weak. It was as if he was falling into an abyss. Ravish reached out and held him up. "Do you want to kill me, Angel, or would you rather kiss me?"

Azrael struggled to make words.

Ravish pulled him even closer and pressed his mouth against his. The kiss was sublime. Azrael was lost. Then he fell. Ravish had let him go. Azrael found himself sitting on the ground.

Ravish was gone. Azrael was enraged. *How dare he?*

From that moment on, Azrael devoted all his time and energy to finding Ravish. He told himself he was pursuing him because he was going to kill him, but deep down, Azrael knew there was more to it than that.

After a while, Michael ordered him to let Ravish go. "There are plenty of demons to destroy," he told him. "Your obsession with Ravish is taking too much time. Forget him. Someone else will take care of him."

Azrael tried to obey, but he couldn't get Ravish out of his mind. His pursuit continued, eventually leading him to The Place In Between.

When Azrael arrived in that dismal place, Hamish, its guardian, was there to greet him. Tall and handsome, Hamish presented an intimidating figure as he regarded Azrael's arrival curiously. "What brings you here, Angel?"

"Am I not welcome? I hear you haven't taken sides, and that you welcome all who seek refuge."

"Yes, but I suspect it is not refuge you are seeking."

"He is here, isn't he?" Azrael pointed at Hamish. "I trust you will not interfere."

"I have no interest in your battle with Ravish," Hamish explained. "However, I will not have your war spilling into this world. If you are looking to take the demon prisoner, then take him and go. If you linger and disturb the order, you will deal with me, Angel."

Azrael lowered his head. "Very well. May I roam freely?"

Hamish floated his hand around the dark and dismal street. "Surrender your sword, then go where you will. Be forewarned, I will not be responsible for your welfare."

"Or for his?" Azrael met his gaze.

"I am not his protector, nor am I yours," Hamish reiterated.

"May I keep my lasso?"

"Certainly, and I will give you back the sword as you leave," Hamish told him.

Azrael watched Hamish walk away. All around him were strange whispers. He was being watched, and he knew his presence there was not being celebrated. He felt threatened and uneasy as he wandered the haunted streets, especially vulnerable without his weapon. "Where are you, Ravish?" He called out. "I know you're here, hiding like the coward you are."

"Looking for me?" Ravish suddenly popped up in front of him, a broad smile on his face. "So nice to see you, my angelic nemesis. I've missed you."

Azrael reached for his sword out of habit then remembered.

"Oops," Ravish said. "Hamish took it. Oh well." He began walking beside him as if they were old friends. "What do you think of this place? Not so bad, with some picture frames and a few throw pillows?"

Azrael shook his head. "You're quite insane. Killing you

wouldn't seem right."

"You didn't come here to kill me, Azrael." His face was close.

Azrael gave him a shove. "I can't kill you here. I promised Hamish. We will go elsewhere." Azrael produced a golden rope which he lassoed around Ravish's wrists and ankles. "You are coming with me."

He knew Ravish couldn't escape. The golden lasso was made to hold demons, especially precocious ones like him.

There were sounds of sorrow as Azrael led his prisoner through the streets.

"Don't worry, my friends," Ravish called out, "we'll come for a visit, after the honeymoon."

"Shut up," Azrael told him. "You won't be coming at all."

"Pity." He smiled. "You do realize what you just said."

"Not everything is sexual in nature, pervert," Azrael retorted.

"It is for me," he replied softly.

Hamish met them at the portal. "I see you found what you came for, Angel."

"I did, and I thank you, Hamish. Come on, Demon. Your time is at hand."

Azrael glanced around the room now at Hamish, Liam, and Ravish. "That's it. As you can see, I didn't succeed in destroying the fiend. He's still here." He looked at Hamish. "Maybe if you hadn't taken my sword."

Ravish smirked. "I assure you he found his sword eventually, just not the one he'd intended."

Azrael scowled. "That's the end of the story. And here we are. I'm surprised you didn't correct everything I said, Demon."

Ravish shrugged. "More or less accurate. Now, may I be permitted to continue our saga?"

"Please do, Ravish." Liam leaned forward. "It was just getting interesting."

Azrael sighed deeply. "Here comes the pornographic version."

Chapter Six: Ravish

"Well, sit back and buckle in, gentleman. You are about to take a wild ride.

"The place Azrael took me was quite romantic. I will try to keep it P.G."

Azrael rolled his eyes. "Romance was not what I had in mind, and it was an old, damp castle."

"Now, don't interrupt." Ravish wagged his finger. "It's only fair."

"You had your turn," Liam said. "Go on, Ravish."

Hamish whispered something in Liam's ear. Liam swatted him.

Ravish grinned. Of course Liam was far more interested in his version. This was the juicy part.

"Whose castle was it?" Hamish asked.

Azrael was about to answer when Ravish put a finger to his own lips. Azrael grumbled but gave Ravish the floor.

"The castle had been built after the Norman Conquest of England. Damn drafty, that place, especially when you're naked."

Ravish was there again in his mind, thoroughly enjoying being Azrael's prisoner. It was strange. He had no fear of the beautiful creature, even if he'd threatened his life multiple times. Not that he doubted Azrael could kill him if he set his mind to it. But somehow being with him, even in those dire circumstances, meant more than his life. And deep down, he knew they'd made a connection.

"I looked in his eyes, and I knew," Ravish said, looking

over at him. "Anyway, Azrael chained my hands to a beam over my head."

"You won't be going anywhere," Azrael had told him. Then he began to undo his shirt.

Ravish eyed him. "Ah, what are you doing, Angel?"

"Undressing you," he said. He took out his sword. Azrael sliced off his shirt with the blade.

"Hey, hey, I liked that shirt. A tailor in France made that for me."

"Well, I hope you're not attached to the trousers either." Azrael unbuttoned Ravish's pants and pulled them down to his ankles, yanking off his boots and tossing his breeches aside.

Ravish narrowed his eyes. He was hanging there completely naked now. "Where exactly is this written in the celestial war manual, Angel Boy?"

Azrael took a step back. "It isn't."

Ravish felt Azrael's gaze sweep over him. It sent shivers down his spine. "Okay. Are you going to stand there and stare at me?"

"If I want to," he said. "Actually demon" — he smiled — "you are mine to do with as I please." He came closer and ran a hand down his chest. "It's a secret fantasy of mine, one I've kept from my brothers."

Ravish smiled. "Please, tell me. I can't wait."

Azrael trailed his hand down Ravish's chest again then took his cock in hand. "To skin a demon alive and see if he screams." Azrael looked up into his eyes.

Ravish laughed. "You're bluffing. That's not your fantasy at all. I can read your thoughts. You want me. You want to touch me and kiss me and feel me inside you. That's your fantasy."

"You are mistaken," Azrael scoffed, taking a few steps

back.

"Kiss me and see," Ravish coaxed.

"I was told you were seductive, to beware."

"I'm not the one who took my clothes off," Ravish grinned. "Kiss me, Angel, unless you're afraid you won't be able to stop."

"I'm not afraid of anything," Azrael retorted, but as he came closer to him, Ravish noticed that he was shaking.

When their lips touched, it was explosive. Azrael moaned against him, and Ravish closed his eyes, wanting nothing more than to hold him. "Let me go, unchain my hands," Ravish pleaded with urgency. "I promise I won't run this time, and I will take you to places you've only dreamed of."

Azrael undid his wrists, and Ravish wrapped his arms around his beautiful angel, taking him down to the cold stone floor. He knew his eyes glowed red as his passion stirred. He lifted Azrael's arms over his head, then slowly undressed him, kissing every inch of his soft, tender skin. He spread his thighs and licked the length of his erect cock as Azrael trembled from need.

Suddenly he pulled Azrael up in his arms, running his hands over him as they kissed passionately. Gently he lifted one of Azrael's wrists, attaching the chain around it.

"What are you—" Azrael gasped.

"Shush," Ravish whispered, lifting the other hand and attaching it as well. Azrael hung there, naked and erect as Ravish circled him. He lowered himself to his haunches, spread Azrael's angelic cheeks, and inserted his tongue deep inside as he reached around to fondle his erection.

Azrael cried out with passion, his hips jutting frantically forward as Ravish replaced his tongue with his cock. As he thrust deep inside of him, Ravish felt something new and sublime. *This is what heaven must feel like.*

"Being inside you," Ravish said, now looking over at

Azrael's shiny eyes filled with tears, "that's where heaven really is."

Ravish didn't even notice that Hamish and Liam had left them alone in the living room.

"Ravish," Azrael whispered, getting to his feet, "I've missed you so much, my devilish man."

Ravish swallowed. "Can this be? Can we finally be together?"

They were now standing face to face.

Azrael was about to reply, but Ravish put up a hand. There were some definite sounds of passion coming from down the hall. He smiled. "Did you?" He looked at his angel.

"Did I?" Azrael tried to look innocent.

"Come on, tell me." Ravish came closer.

"I might have tweaked a little. I figure I owed them something. I could care less about Hamish's soul."

Ravish laughed. "Okay."

"You know . . ." Azrael reached out and touched his cheek. "You left me hanging there in that castle. I don't know if I can ever forgive you for that."

"I'm sorry, Azrael. I have always regretted that. Until Hamish and Liam, I didn't think it was possible that we were possible. Do you forgive me? I know I have a lot to make up for."

"Well, you can start by kissing me, Demon boy." Azrael grinned as Ravish pulled him into his arms. "Unless you're afraid you won't be able to stop."

Ravish paused and met his gaze. He laughed. "Touché, Angel Cake," he said, and smothered his angel's mouth with his.

CHAPTER SEVEN: LIAM

It was Liam who had pulled Hamish out of the living room. As Ravish began to tell them what happened after Azrael brought him to the castle, something in the room changed. Everyone was feeling it. Azrael suddenly couldn't take his eyes off Ravish. He seemed to be reliving every moment, and as he did, Ravish, too, was focused on the Angel.

"I began to feel like a voyeur in there," Liam told Hamish in the bedroom.

"Me too," Hamish said.

"And you know what else I'm feeling?" Liam raised an eyebrow then started to undo Hamish's shirt.

"Oh, okay," Hamish said as Liam began to undo his pants.

"I want you naked now," Liam told him.

"Ooh, I like this." Hamish swallowed.

"If I had a golden lasso," Liam said, sinking down to take off Hamish shoes and pants, "I'd hogtie you."

"You don't need to," Hamish said, kissing his neck. "I'll do whatever you want."

Liam licked his lips. "Really? Whatever I want?"

"Sure." Hamish smiled. "Name it."

Liam didn't undress. Instead, he went over, reclined on the bed and propped himself up on two pillows. He was hard, and for some reason, he was staying that way. He shouldn't overthink it. He looked at his man. "Damn, you are so hot. Put your hands behind your head."

Hamish did as he'd asked, smiling at him.

"Thrust out your hips. Um, like that." Liam reached his

hands inside his pants and began to handle his own cock then he unzipped his pants and lifted out his erection. It seemed so long since he'd wanted Hamish like this. He could hardly breathe. He pulled his pants down all the way, displaying himself to Hamish.

Hamish stood still, patiently looking at him.

"Turn around," Liam urged. "I want to see that beautiful ass."

When Hamish turned, Liam let his gaze trail over his broad back. He couldn't see the openings anymore. He turned his attention to the generous swell of his ass with the sweet little hollows on each side. "Okay, look at me, baby."

Hamish turned again. "Please, now?"

"Soon. Your cock is even harder. Tell me," Liam said, pulling off his t-shirt and rubbing his nipples, "what do you want to do to me?"

"I want to fuck you so hard," Hamish said softly, his voice shaking. "I want to suck your nipples and your cock and hold you in my arms. I love you so much. I want you, Liam. I've missed you so much. Please. Now?"

Liam opened his arms and went up on his knees. He pulled Hamish down to the bed, kissing him, reaching over with his free hand to get the lube and condoms out from the nightstand.

Their lovemaking was fast and furious. Hamish inside him again was emotional, and Liam felt the tears pour down his face. It was like the pain, the fear, the memories of the past faded away in Hamish's arms.

Later as he lay there with him, Liam said, "I couldn't feel the opening in your shoulder blades anymore. Is that good?" Liam touched his hair.

"It's not bad." Hamish kissed his nose.

"Did you do it, did you take the anxiety away?" He felt

whole again, and he knew he'd no longer need the pills.

Hamish met his gaze. "No." He glanced at the door. "I think Azrael did that."

"Did you ask him to do it?" Liam deposited tiny kisses on Hamish's shoulder.

"No, but Azrael has the power to heal psychic pain."

"But I remember everything," Liam said. "It just feels different. That panicky feeling is gone."

"He left the memories." Hamish kissed his forehead. "I'm not sure how, but he did. It's like he removed the ulcer but left the leg."

"It's quiet out there. Do you think they've left?" Liam asked. "I'd really like to thank him."

Hamish got out of bed and went to the window. "Look."

Liam came to join him. The beautiful leaves were still there, but there was no barrier.

Liam walked over and put on his robe, then slipped back into Hamish's arms. "You need to put clothes on before I drag you back to bed."

Hamish tickled him. "Any time, baby."

"I'm going to check and see if they are still out there." Liam left the room and looked around. They were gone. "Hamish?"

Hamish came out into the living room, belting his robe. "They're gone, eh?"

Liam looked at him. "You knew."

He nodded.

"What about your soul?"

"I told you," Hamish said. "My soul belongs to me." Hamish pulled Liam into his arms and kissed him hotly. "And my heart belongs to you."

Liam undid Hamish's robe and took Hamish's cock in his hand. "Your big, hard, cock belongs to me too. It's mine, right?"

Hamish smiled at him. "Every inch of it."

"So, what do you think happened?" Liam asked curiously as Hamish propelled him back toward the bedroom.

"I guess they had better things to do." Hamish kissed him passionately on the mouth then pulled off Liam's robe.

"Um," Liam moaned against Hamish, his hand tightening on Hamish's cock as he felt his lovers' hands roam over his ass. "And, from the looks of it, so do we."

ABOUT THE SUEDE DELRAY

Suede is an award winning, bestselling author. She has written many academic articles on delinquency, racism and homophobia, as well as numerous romantic, mystery and fantasy novels. Recently she took an early retirement from her job in law enforcement where she worked with juveniles, to devote herself to her first love, writing. Suede lives with her loving partner of many years and their pets. She enjoys travelling, reading about current events, debating, and walking.

Red Run Ruckus

By

Lynn Michaels

When pushed to the brink of extinction, you stand and fight —
even if you're a red deer shifter.

An extended search for more red deer shifters results in some
success and a celebration of Mabon, the fall equinox, and a
great feast at Donner's estate. When the feast is attacked by
the wolves, Donner is ready to fight back and defend his family at all cost. But Rory, his mate, won't let Donner take on the
wolves alone.

DEDICATION

To all the shifter-loving readers who've followed this story through the seasons. I hope you all enjoy the rest of the ride.

RED RUN RUCKUS

Donner's heart filled to bursting when he took in the sight of so many deer at his table. This year had been incredible. He'd always imagined he would die alone — the old king stag of nothing. Then he'd met Rory, and his whole world changed. Their love and their children, and even finding their first addition to their herd, Emma, who birthed Maja less than a month after their twins were born, had convinced Donner to extend the search for others. Emma had been pregnant and about to give birth in deer-form when they first found her. She'd lost her mate, and she'd been difficult to track down. Most deer went into hiding when the wolves had decided to slaughter their race. They would be hard to find, but he and Rory had found Emma. Then they'd found others. There would be more.

They had added to their herd in a remarkable way when no one believed it could happen, especially those on the council who knew damned well what the wolves were up to with their *mutocide* — coined from the Latin for shift combined with the Latin suffix for killing, as in *genocide* for shifters. Despite the wolves' insanity, not one but two new stags sat at his table. In addition to himself and his mate, Rory, he now had Eryk and Rocco. Both were big with the broad shoulders common in red deer shifters.

Donner raised his glass and tapped it with a butter knife, getting everyone's attention. "I can't tell you all how happy I am. My table is full, as it should be."

"Hear, hear! Fitting for a king." Isla called, raising her

glass. She had also joined their herd. She was an old hind — as old as the wind.

"Thank you." Donner nodded in acknowledgment of her praise. "I hope to be the kind of king you all will continue to support in the years to come."

Everyone cheered. The years to come were not promised to them, but the words held hope. Donner sat in the seat next to Rory. Rory slid his hand over Donner's thigh with a promise of a private celebration later.

The children sat at a separate table. With six adults taking up the big one, having them at a smaller table was convenient. They were still close by, since no one wanted to let them out of their sight for a moment.

Pride warmed him as he watched his daughter, Alana, tending to the youngest of them, Lotte. It was good to see the youth eating with gusto. He was too young and malnourished, having lost his birthing parent, Mikel, before he arrived with his father, Eryk. A haunting sadness surrounded both of them, lingering much longer than he'd hoped. Donner didn't even want to contemplate what losing a mate would be like. He squeezed Rory's leg, needing the solid feel of his muscle to reassure him.

Rory smiled up at him. "The food is delicious. Emma and Isla did a great job." They'd not only prepared the delicious food, but they also did a marvelous job decorating for Mabon. The candles glowed, warming the atmosphere and complimenting the fall colors of various golds and yellow with brown and dark green accents. Maple leaves, apples and pears, and various squash adorned their table. A pumpkin the children had helped decorate had been placed in the center. They celebrated the bounty of the harvest feast, which meant not only food but family, and also the balance of light and dark. Winter would be there soon, covering the land with snow, but for the moment, they would enjoy the cooler winds of autumn.

Their feast was incredible. They had everything imaginable. A rich pumpkin soup, sweet potatoes, an amazing roasted turkey, and a full basket of Mabon bread were strewn across the table. For dessert, they had their choice of pies — pumpkin, pecan, or apple. There was also a large tin of spice cookies on the kitchen counter. The bounty was fit for a king and his court.

Donner glanced over at their children, Finley and Alana. It'd been nearly a year since their birth, and they were growing up so fast. Shifter children aged as their deer side, not their human side, even in human form. They'd spent most of their time learning everything Rory could teach them in days rather than years. As humans, they now presented as moody pre-teens. Alana almost always walked around with a saucy attitude, and Finley moped constantly.

It was glorious seeing them interact with the newest deer, Lotte, who was only a few months old, and Maja, who they treated like a sister. They'd witnessed her birth when they were only a few weeks old. Donner didn't know how much they remembered of that time. For them, Maja had always been there. As it should be with deer. The larger the family, the better. Their six adults and four children made Donner happy and hopeful his herd would continue to grow.

A loud shattering of glass interrupted their meal. Donner jerked upright and cautiously hurried toward the sound, his new bucks Eryk and Rocco behind him. Rory gathered the children, shushing them so the adults could hear. Donner ignored them, focusing on the danger. Ready to protect his family.

In the sitting room, he found a large stone had been thrown through the front window. The glass and frame, now destroyed, had been several hundred years old. Before the anger and sadness over it could take hold of his heart, figures silhouetted on the front lawn moved toward the house.

By the dark mother! It was wolves. "Eryk, tell Rory to get the kids in the basement. Rocco, out the east side. I'll take the west." They needed to flank the enemy and ensure none were sneaking in from the sides, but the bulk of the pack were coming straight on to the front. "Come back here with Rory once the women and children are safe."

All three bucks ran. The children would be safe below with Isla and Emma for the moment, but if they didn't stop the wolves, that wouldn't last.

As Donner headed out to flank the west, he tapped the screen of his cell phone. They needed reinforcements. In a few rings, Martin Silva answered. "Donner?"

He popped it to speaker and breathed out, "Wolves. Here."

"How many?" Martin sounded pissed. He growled a little before cursing. "Damn Pritchard!" Martin was the head of the council and a wolverine shifter—no relation to Pritchard, the wolf king, and his bastard hounds. Martin had proved a solid ally in this war.

"Don't know. Maybe a dozen. There's going to be a fight."

"On my way!"

Donner was out of time. After he disconnected, he tucked the phone back in his pocket and ripped off his clothes, leaving them wherever they fell. Then he shifted. His regal antlers stretched out from his head. Arms and legs melded into dangerous weapons of pure muscle that ended in sharp hooves. He galloped into the fray without hesitation.

He was on the wolves in seconds. These weren't the scrawny survivors he'd fought over the past year to get where they were. No, these were healthy, strong beasts with speed and agility and teeth. Very sharp teeth. They'd brought the fight to the deer, and Donner would end it. He lowered his head, goring two in their sides, simultaneously. He jumped and turned, kicking out with hind legs to crack a couple of skulls. He fought with madness and fury.

Donner glanced across the lawn. The setting sun made it difficult to see, but Eryk was closest to him and holding his own. He stood almost as tall as Donner, his rack nearly as full, and he used similar tactics to stab with his antlers and smash with his hooves. The double toed hoof of a deer wasn't exactly made for fighting, but it got the job done.

He leaped over an attacker. It turned and snapped at his flanks. He could outrun it, but he no longer considered running an option. He wanted the wolf dead. *How dare they attack on the holy Mabon, the autumn feast?*

Donner lowered his head to attack again. He heard Rory's bellow in the distance—unmistakable. His mate would be giving them hell. Rory was a gorgeous red deer, true to their breed. Not as tall as Donner, even in deer form, but he was stocky and solid. He maneuvered around the pack, managing to capture a few wolves between them. They charged together.

They were causing a lot of damage to the pack relatively quickly, but it wasn't enough. A dozen more wolves loped up the field into the fray. Donner had only a second to worry about them before a snarling beast charged him. Rory danced to the side and body checked it at the last second. Then it caught Donner's hoof to the side of its head.

The sun had nearly set when another bellow echoed through the night. One of the others was in trouble. Donner and Rory fought side by side toward the center of the battle, but they couldn't help their herdsman. If one of them fell, it would be over fast. Donner sent a quick prayer to the Child of Light to hold his new family safe.

In the distance, he heard the roar of engines, maybe a truck. *Is it Martin, or more wolves?* He couldn't do anything about it. He had to keep his head in the fight.

Two trucks drove up the small road leading to Donner's estate. His heart pounded furiously in his chest with uncertainty, hoping it was Martin with reinforcements. Donner turned and struck another wolf. He was ready for more, poised with his antlers in attack mode.

Blood spilled across the battered lawn as if the ground were another casualty, with the dirt and grass upturned and wolf bodies scattered over it, making it hard to maneuver.

A gunshot rent the air. Silence loomed in the echo. A man stepped out onto the lawn. More joined behind him. "We're all armed!" Martin called out.

Donner expelled a loud breath in relief.

"If you're canine and able to move, you better get your ass out of here in the next three seconds, or we'll fill it full of lead." He cocked his shotgun back, reloaded, and slammed it back in place. The clicks snapped out to reinforce his words. At first, an unnatural stillness surrounded them. Nobody moved. "One."

The remaining wolves scrambled for the woods and the road, leaving many bodies both injured and dead behind. Martin directed his men to take care of the dead and the injured, moving both to the waiting trucks.

Rory shifted back to his muscular human form and ran across the lawn, avoiding the worst of the casualties. Donner quickly followed.

Rocco had been injured badly and was set up in the living room. He'd broken a bone in his leg. Shifters healed much differently than humans. He needed to keep it immobile for a minimum of twelve hours before shifting. That alone would heal it, making casting unnecessary for such a short time, but he needed to be still for it to align properly.

Rory bumped into Donner's shoulder and raised his eyebrows as Emma tended to him.

"I know." Donner had other things to worry about besides Emma's interest in the buck. The attack had been a declaration of war. He left Rory to look after the herd and proceeded to corner Martin near the garden shed. "What are you doing out here?"

"We need to tend to your yard. It's . . . destroyed. Bloody."

"You need to tend to the wolves." Donner crossed his arms over his chest. The anger he'd been suppressing since the stone had crashed through his front window coursed through him like a flashover of flames in a tight room.

"We took care of it."

"No. I mean Pritchard and the rest of them. Didn't we create the council to stop this kind of thing from happening? The wolves have committed mutocide multiple times. The lions almost totally eradicated the hyenas—"

"We stopped all that. There's been peace." He threw his hands up in obvious exasperation.

"Not anymore." Donner grabbed a heavy-duty rake with metal tines. "I can kind of understand the lion-hyena conflict. They're competitors. But in the wild, nature's wolves do not destroy the herd. They'd lose their food source if they did. But not shifters. They don't actually *eat* other shifters. They're simply pricks."

Martin took the rake. "I get it. I hate this. We risked sanction bringing guns here."

"I can't blame you. It was the only way to get them to stop."

"I know you're right. About all of it. I'm working on something."

"While you're working on it. I'm preparing to take Pritchard down. This is my family. One I've worked hard for. Suffered for. I'm not letting him get away with this." Donner punched the air between them with his index finger, pointing at Martin. Neither Martin or the others were at fault, but it didn't matter—his anger wanted a target. "Fucking wolves. This time they went too far."

Donner walked back into the main house, searching for Rory. When he found him, he grabbed Rory by the shoulders and pulled him into a hug. He needed comfort from his mate, and he bet Rory needed it, too. "Let's go to bed. There's nothing else we can do for now."

Martin had sent guards to walk the perimeter, but it didn't ease Donner's tension much. He led Rory up the stairs to their room. The twins had since moved to a different wing of the house where they could have separate bedrooms. Rory had been sad about it, but Alana wanted more privacy. They had to support that. Luckily, their home was large enough for all their new family to fill the empty rooms.

Their suite occupied most of the center of the second floor. A comfortable sitting area and a big king-sized bed, where he led Rory, framed the huge fireplace that centered the room. He yanked the covers off, then slowly undressed his mate. Rory's auburn hair shimmered in the low light, and Donner plunged his hands through it. Rory grunted when Donner tugged. He needed them to be closer, and he bet Rory did too.

He pulled his mate to him, pressing their bodies together, and blew a breath into his hair. "Rory . . ."

Rory's arms came around Donner's waist. "I'm here. We're both here. Relax." Rory stretched up for a kiss. He took Donner's mouth gently, sucking on his lips, then giving him a quick peck.

Donner went in for more. Another peck. A flick of his tongue. They both opened their mouths, pressing together, quickly brushing their tongues, then pulling back. They danced — teased. He loved Rory for the tender and taunting love, but he was ready for more.

He pulled his shirt off and dropped his pants to the floor while Rory also undressed. He pressed Rory against him again, but this time they were naked. The skin on Rory's shoulders was smooth and covered in freckles. Donner bent to kiss them.

Rory shivered. "Let's get in bed."

Donner agreed readily and sat on the edge. He remembered the first time they came together when they'd first met. The rut had consumed them, pushing them to the mating, but so much more kept them together. Yes, the twins, but beyond that, Donner cared for this man. Rory drove him crazy in all the best ways. They'd progressed quickly in their relationship, as deer tended to do, but they hadn't sacrificed richness and quality. He knew who Rory was, and Rory knew him.

Rory tucked his nose in the crook of Donner's neck, then licked his collar bone. He moved to the hollow of Donner's throat, trailing open mouth kisses across his skin. He swung his leg over Donner's thighs to straddle him. Donner showed his appreciation by cupping Rory's ass in his hands and squeezing. Rory clenched his ass, then rolled his hips. Their cocks were smashed together and growing harder and more uncomfortable by the second.

He slid Rory to the side and back to the mattress to get a hand on both of them. He wrapped his fingers around Rory's dick, pressing it against his, then he humped against his gorgeous cock. He tightened his hold, and Rory moaned. Donner's desire bubbled up from deep below, hinting at the rut that would surely come this spring. It hadn't happened this past year, because both Rory and Emma had young. They were older now, and the coming spring would bring more babies. He longed for it.

Rory reached around and squeezed Donner's ass. He mewled in Donner's ear. It sent a chill up his spine. "Donner . . ." Rory almost never acted needy. When he wanted something, he took it. Even though he'd birthed their fawns, he was still every bit the strong buck, ready to challenge. Having carried their children only made Rory stronger. Unlike the natural deer, all shifter deer stuck together and were led by royalty, but Rory made a fit mate for a king. If anything happened to Donner, he'd be an amazing leader. Nothing turned him on like Rory's intensity and strength.

Donner let go of his hold and pushed up to look at Rory's face, all sexed out with passion—lids low, mouth open, cheeks pink. His freckles stood out more when he looked like that. He kissed Rory again, enjoying the slide of tongues. He pushed Rory's thick, red hair back from his face. "What do you want?" Donner would bottom for him, but Rory normally chose to.

"Bottom. Please." He pressed his cock into Donner's hip.

"You sure? I can?"

"Need you. In me. Around me. Holding me. Please."

Donner wouldn't argue. Everything Rory gave him was a blessing. He grabbed the lube and worshiped Rory's cock and balls while prepping him, until Rory bucked his hips. "Damn! Stop teasing, Donner." He huffed.

Donner chuckled and pushed Rory's legs back, tilting his ass up as he knee-walked closer. He knelt behind Rory and lined his cock up with his hole, then pushed in. He took a few strokes, then grabbed one of Rory's feet to spread him wider. He pumped his hips furiously. Rory blinked a few times, then stroked his cock with a long moan.

"Yes, Rory. Come for me." Donner watched him jack off, keeping up his own pace.

Rory came hard, shooting out over his chest and abs while calling out. The erotic sight pushed Donner forward to his orgasm—like lightning. It shot through his body, leaving little prickly sensations behind as it went.

They cleaned up. Then they spent some time cuddled up together with the lights off. "Are you happy, Rory?" Donner asked in the safety of the darkness.

"I am. Way more than I thought I'd be." He rubbed Donner's shoulder, comforting and soothing him. "When I first came here, I was terrified."

"You didn't seem like it to me. Ha! You were so brave. Unbelievably brave, Rory."

"On the outside."

"You've never told me that."

Rory moved with a shrug. "Who wouldn't have been scared? I mean, I came here alone. You were a stranger. But . . ." He sighed, happily. "An extremely attractive stranger."

"The feeling was mutual." Donner laughed. "And what about now?"

"I love our herd. I love Emma and the kids." He shuffled around. "I'm still wary of the bucks—"

"That's natural." He pulled Rory in tighter. He didn't want him to worry.

"I know. I feel awful with Rocco hurt. But my inner deer still struggled against leaving him in Emma's care." Rory had helped birth Emma's fawn. He was very protective of both of them.

"Things have a way of working out."

"I know. But I have a more important question." He sounded hesitant.

"Ask me anything, Rory. You know you can. Always."

"What are we going to do about the wolves?"

Nothing was settled. Donner wanted to declare war officially. Wanted to eradicate the wolf problem from the inside out. In fact, he'd placed a call to a vulture shifter who specialized in, well . . . taking people out. Or shifters, as the case might be. Donner wanted them all out, but he settled for putting the hit out on Prichard. If a better leader took over the pack, maybe that new wolf would end their issues.

He pulled on his sweatpants and a t-shirt and jogged down the stairs. Rory and Emma were feeding the kids leftovers of turkey sandwiches and sweet potatoes from the feast for lunch. Alana was obviously sulking as she sifted through her food without eating much.

"What's going on?" All eyes lifted to him.

Alana set her fork on the table in front of her. "It's not fair, papa." Her accent was a strange mix of the Scottish and American of her parents. She shoved her long red hair, obviously inherited from Rory, behind her ears.

"What's not fair, darling?" Donner bent over and kissed her forehead, but that only made her huff in protest.

"Daddy says I have to share a room if we get more deer."

"If you don't, where's everyone going to sleep?"

She looked down at her food with a scowl. "I didn't think about that. But I don't want a room with Fin. He snores. Ouch." She bent and rubbed her leg. Finley had kicked her under the table. For twins, they sure fought a lot.

Rory stepped in. "Now stop. I suspect you'll share with Maja and maybe another, if we have more little girls."

Donner saw Emma off to the side, smothering a smile. Donner raised an eyebrow, but she only shrugged.

Maja had declared herself the minder of babies, wanting little Lotte to room with them, which started another row with Alana.

Emma handed Donner a plate with a sandwich, salad, and her baked pears, which he loved, on it. "You'll need your strength for this crew." She nodded to the table where the kids were eating.

"No lie, *droch isean*. All of them!" Donner joked, calling them brats. They were good kids going through some growing pains. He took his plate and sat between Alana and Finley, smiling at both of them.

Everyone settled into their meal, and even Alana was eating. The other adults were around the house. Eryk had taken Lotte upstairs to play, and Rocco was still on the couch with his injured leg. Isla was probably taking a nap as well, which made Donner contemplate naps for everyone, especially him and Rory.

Then a gunshot exploded, and everyone jumped. The children's' eyes all grew wide.

A second shot.

"Get them below. Go on." Donner rushed them, but Rory and Emma had already started guiding the children away.

"Where's Lotte?" Maja called out, refusing to go to the basement without the littlest of them.

Emma nudged her. "Come on. Eryk will bring the babe."

Donner pulled his phone out of his pocket and texted Martin. In seconds, Martin replied.

Wolf shot near the barn.

The barn was an extension of his house that he'd created for having babies. *How'd they get so close?* Shifters always gave birth in animal form, and deer were extremely vulnerable at that time. He'd made it a sanctuary. It was where his children and Maja were all born and where Donner hoped they'd have more fawns the next year. He was angry at the wolves for invading and tarnishing it. He shook himself out of that line of thought. There was no time for it. He typed a furious reply. *How many?*

Only two. One injured. The other fled.

By all rights, they both should have been dead, but the guards had done their job by stopping them. Martin was sacrificing a lot to have armed men stationed there. Whether the council admitted it or not, they were in a war, and Donner wasn't about to fight fair.

Two of Martin's men had moved the captured wolf inside to tend his wound. He'd been shot in the shoulder. The sight of him patched up and sleeping in their birthing stall made Donner want to growl—something deer never did. It was a complete invasion of their most personal spaces. *Bastard wolves!*

"Where's Martin?" He checked his phone again. It'd been too long since he'd received the text stating Martin was on his way.

His men gave each other looks of frustration. "He'll be here," one said.

Donner grunted at them and walked outside to wait. Staring at the wolf would only get him more worked up. He pressed his shoulders against the side of the building and crossed his arms over his chest. There was no sign of Martin, but Rory stalking toward him across the backfield was a welcome sight. "Hey. How're the kids?"

"Fine. Emma's starting them on new lessons today. That'll distract them."

"Good."

"If you say so."

Donner had nothing else to say about it. The situation frustrated him beyond belief, but it was also scary. He grabbed Rory and pulled him into his arms as much to comfort Rory as himself.

Before long, a huge animal crawled from the woods—a wolverine with a band of light fur running across its body between the spot on its back, feet, and stomach which were black as night. His snout was the same black with a halo of the lighter fur around its ears. Unlike a natural wolverine, this one wore a satchel tied to its neck. When it got close enough, it shifted into the human form of Martin.

Rory groaned and hid his eyes, then darted into the barn.

"Donner." Martin nodded in greeting. "I have news."

"Here." Rory came out with a towel and handed it to Martin.

"Thanks." Martin wrapped the towel around his waist. Nakedness never bothered Donner. It was part of who they were as shifters, but the weather was turning colder. With the leaves falling from the trees, winter would be coming soon.

Martin might have been a little chilly, but he suspected Rory had other motivations for wanting the older man to cover up. Once Martin fastened the towel securely, he continued. "As I was saying . . .we have news."

"I hope it's a sanction against the wolves."

"Yes and no."

Donner jerked forward. "What?" He wanted to strangle the *no* out of him.

Rory grabbed his arm, holding him back. "Let the man speak."

Donner huffed, then held his hand out in acquiescence.

"Donner, we have to meet as a full council to make it official. You must be there, but we also do *not* want to pull you away from your home and family at a time like this."

"I don't want to delay things."

"You won't. If we can meet here, that is."

Donner was about to agree quickly, but Martin looked too sheepish at the moment. "What aren't you telling us?"

"The council, particularly the predators, don't want to sanction *all* the wolves." Martin actually cringed.

Rory huffed. "What's the proposal?"

Martin looked around, then sighed. "They want to sanction Prichard and name a new wolf to the council."

"That won't dispel him as king." Donner paced the floor. It wasn't enough.

"No, but if someone else represents the wolves, maybe they can influence the others away from Prichard. Might even choose to challenge him."

"If this new guy lost a challenge, we'd be right back where we began." Donner's patience was nearly at an end.

Martin touched his arm. "We have to take it one step at a time. If the councilman lost a challenge, it still wouldn't bring Prichard back as representative. But we're playing what-if games. The only thing we can do right now is bring them here and agree Prichard is out. It's the first step. We take the rest as it comes."

Donner wanted to argue, but Rory rubbed against his side. "Donner. Martin's right. Let's bring them here. Have the meeting. Then we'll move forward. Maybe a new wolf will help change things."

Donner gave a curt nod. They were right, but he didn't want them to be. "Call them. Bring them here." They needed to move forward quickly.

Martin fiddled with his satchel, pulling out his phone, then made a call. Donner turned away and walked back across the field. The kids were dying to get out and play as deer, but with this threat, they'd been kept inside. If his vulture associate could take Prichard out, though, maybe a new wolf might change things for the better. It would have to be someone brave. He considered the wolf who'd let them walk away, giving them a chance, when he and Rory first met. It needed to be someone like him, someone capable of seeing the deer as strong and courageous and worthy.

He headed into his office on the first floor of the house and pulled out his phone and placed a call to the vulture to check-in. "Status?" he asked when the line picked up.

"Target located. I'm formulating a plan. I can implement in six hours. Do I have a go-ahead?"

Donner didn't want any of the other details. He trusted the vulture as much as anyone could trust a vulture. "Go ahead. Text me a sunshine emoji when it's done."

The line went dead.

Donner turned around to see Rory glaring at him from the doorway. "Who were you talking to? What are they doing?"

"You don't want to know." He tucked his phone in his pocket.

"Donner. Come on. We share everything. If you leave me in the dark, how can I have your back?"

"You don't need to have my back. You need to be safe."

Rory looked down and scratched the doorframe with the toe of his sneaker. "That's not how it works. We talked about this." He spoke softly, making his determination clear.

Donner had agreed that they needed to be on the same team when they had rescued Emma. Rory had to be a part of the planning and execution. He had to be included, or they wouldn't be effective.

Finally Donner gave in. "Fine. An associate of mine. No one you should know. He's going to help us take care of this wolf problem."

"He's helping us how?" Rory grabbed Donner's arms, squeezing them a little.

"He's going to take out Prichard."

Rory let go of his arms. "That makes us better than them, how?"

"It's not about being better. They threatened my family. I'm ending it in any way I can."

Rory shook his head. He looked disappointed, but Donner wouldn't give in on this one.

Two days later, the council arrived. Rory was still angry at him, but he was coming around. If the new wolf was promising, maybe it would help with the war and with Rory's anger.

Rocco had healed enough to be able to move around. He insisted on taking up a guard position with Eryk outside the house. They shifted to deer form, allowing them to move around with a bit more stealth, and if something was amiss, their bellows would be clearly heard.

Emma and Isla took the children upstairs to the large playroom they'd created in the center of the upper floor. The main fireplace centered the room, but on the third floor, it didn't need to be used often, only on the coldest of days. It made it a perfect place for the kids to play and hang out.

Ferdinand, Donner's pet mouse, stayed up in that room most of the time. He loved the children. Between playing with Ferdinand and the recently added video game consuls, the kids would be completely occupied.

That allowed Rory to play host with him and gave Donner another opportunity to be proud of the mate he'd chosen. Rory put their disagreement behind him and welcomed the shifters into their home. They sat everyone around the large table in the big formal dining room. It sat a dozen people, but there were more than that on the council, so they'd brought in extra chairs.

Rory made sure the predators didn't take up all the spots along the table, making way for others. Donner brought out refreshments, adding them to the table and the sideboard. Everyone chatted peacefully while they waited for Martin to show up, escorting his new wolf.

Donner was at once happy and nervous. To see everyone, predator and prey alike, getting along was amazing. But tension slowly started building as the minutes ticked by, causing him to worry.

Soon the doorbell chimed, and Rory went to answer it. Moments later, he walked Martin into the dining room, followed by a stout young man who appeared to be in his human-thirties, which could make him nearly a hundred years old or more. Not as old as Donner and Martin, but older than some of the others.

Martin cleared his throat. "Some of you may know Brayton. Others maybe not. He's a high-ranking wolf from the coast. He's interested in promoting business interests, economics. That sort of thing."

Brayton stepped forward and nodded to those in the room. "Doesn't matter to me what kind you are. We're all shifters. We all have to live in this world. I'd rather we made it a better place. That's not going to happen unless we work together."

He had shaggy brown hair with gray spots near his temples and narrow, intelligent eyes.

Orji, the matriarch of the largest lion pride represented, stood up. Her skin was ebony, while her long hair was the golden wheat of her cat. She held her shoulders back and paused, ensuring everyone was listening. "And do you fear going against your leader? Prichard is a powerful shifter."

"He is. He has a huge following, and I know this will split the pack." He took another step into the room. "I'm not without my own followers. And . . . I suspect this move would gain me even more. There are many who would rather back me, who are afraid of Prichard and his loyal wolves."

"And what are we to expect with war between wolves?" someone asked, but Donner didn't catch who.

"Better than what we're getting now," another voice spoke up, and the crowd began talking amongst themselves, creating a ruckus.

Martin pulled out a large rock from his pocket and banged it on the table. "Listen. Order." The rock belonged to the head of the council and was passed to each new leader to be used as a token of respect and peace among us. Everyone quieted once it was out, and the meeting officially came to order.

Donner nodded at Rory to step out. Even though he was Donner's mate, he wasn't part of the council. He left the room, and Donner looked to Martin to continue.

"We're here to vote Prichard out and vote Brayton in. The fall out will be what it is, and we can deal with it as we go forward. The war on the deer must stop. It's not only Donner's red deer suffering. Different deer shifters across the globe struggle with the wolves' vicious pursuits. If lions and hyenas can sit at the table together, so can wolf and deer."

Orji glanced at the hyena leader across the room, but the hyena ignored her. Donner would take indifference over aggression.

Martin tapped the rock twice on the table to open the floor to questions. "Any relevant questions?"

They had all been briefed on the topic, so no one spoke up. Martin held the rock in the air, calling for one last request to speak. When no one did, he tapped the rock twice more. "We vote. Everyone, stand."

Everyone stood up with chairs scratching across the hardwood floor. A few were already standing, but they would sit on the floor if needed once Martin called the vote.

"All in favor of this change, please sit. Those opposed, remain standing."

Almost everyone sat down. The few who did not surprised Donner. Closely related species, the red fennec and artic fox stood. Donner didn't hold it against them. Loyalty was only part of it—fear, the other. Several rabbits and sheep also stayed standing, afraid of going against Prichard and having him redirect his target to them.

Donner didn't blame them, but they were wrong. He cleared his throat. "Once Prichard is finished with the deer, where do you think he'll go next?"

Martin tapped his rock on the table. "You missed your time for questions, Donner. Even though you have a good one."

Two rabbits sat. They had the majority without them, but changing their minds was a more important win.

Two bird species argued in the back of the room until, with a huff, they both sat.

"Anyone else changing their vote?" Martin asked. No one moved. "For the record. We're recording those voting no. However, the majority is yes. Brayton now represents the wolves on the council." Martin turned and shook Brayton's hand. Everything went back to being normal and joyous.

Then Brayton turned to face Donner. He smiled, but it looked far more smug than expected. His eyes narrowed suspiciously. The change was a huge power-move for Brayton, even within his part of the pack, but the larger wolf hierarchy as well. It positioned him to challenge Prichard, and he might win. Donner hoped the vulture would make it so they'd never have to find out.

After everyone left, the house seemed quiet and spacious. Donner breathed a sigh of relief, then helped Rory get the house back in order. They ate, then went upstairs to watch a movie with the kids. They piled onto the couch, and Ferdinand even snuggled up with Finley. Half of them were asleep by the time the movie ended.

Ferdinand scampered off to his bed, while Donner helped get Alana and Finley tucked into theirs. They both balked at goodnight kisses. Donner missed the days when they loved nothing more than spending time with them, cuddling or playing. Mostly, they wanted to be left alone outside of their lessons now. Sometimes being a parent was easy, and sometimes it wasn't, but seeing his young deer thriving made it worth every second.

He shut the light off with a sigh then followed Rory back to their room. Rory sat on the bed and scowled. Donner had to get things worked out between them. "Rory? I'm sorry."

He blew out a hard breath. "It's fine."

"It's not. You're still mad." Donner got on his knees in front of Rory, shuffling between his legs. He wrapped his hands around Rory's waist and put his head against his thigh.

Rory scrubbed through Donner's thick hair. "I get it. What you're doing. I'm pissed you didn't talk to me about it first."

Donner worried his forehead over Rory's knee. "I know. I'm sorry. I'm used to taking charge and making decisions. Used to being alone."

"You're not. Not anymore, and not ever again." Rory ran his fingers through Donner's hair. "We have other deer to think about. Alana and Fin, yeah, but Maja and Lotte and their parents. You don't get to make a bunch of decisions without talking to us."

"You're right. I'll do better."

Rory tugged on Donner's hair, tilting his head back with it. "You better." Then he bent forward and kissed Donner's waiting lips. A gentle caress of flesh. Then he pulled back. Mischief sparkled in his deep, mahogany eyes. "I think you need to make it up to me." He raised an eyebrow and smirked.

"I think you're right. Let's start here." He unbuckled Rory's belt, unfastened his pants. "These slacks are nice, and you looked great for the council, but they're gone now."

Rory lifted his ass up, and Donner pulled them off, sliding the fabric along his thighs. Soft auburn hair covered his legs. With the pants shoved to the floor, he pulled Rory's briefs off to join them. His beautiful uncut cock filled, jutting up, waiting for him. Donner pulled on his foreskin and licked at the tip. Rory wiggled and gasped. Donner repeated his movement before taking Rory's dick into his mouth. He slid up and down, hollowing his cheeks as he sucked.

Rory stopped wiggling. He bucked his hips up as Donner sucked. Rory moaned and dug his fingers into Donner's shoulder. The gentle kneading encouraged Donner to keep going. He cupped Rory's balls, squeezing and massaging. Slobber dripped over Rory's dick. Donner wiped it with his fingers then slid them back behind Rory's balls. Rory slid forward, lifting his ass and spreading his legs to give Donner more access. Rory loved to be teased, so he slid his finger over Rory's hole, only letting the very tip push in.

He sucked harder, rubbing along the edge and tapping on his hole in a sensual torment. Then he pressed harder, easing a bit more than the tip inside.

Rory came hard. It tasted a little salty and a bit acidic like limes, but it was perfect for Donner. It was Rory, and he loved his taste. After he took all Rory had to give, he nuzzled his nose in Rory's groin. He might have stayed there longer, but his cock was hard, pressing tightly against his pants. He stood up and dropped them, briefs and all.

"You need some help?" Rory asked. He reached around Donner and grabbed his ass, yanking him forward. He hummed as he took Donner's cock into his mouth.

"Fuck, Rory . . . your mouth is so hot." Donner punched his hips forward then pulled back with a moan. Rory bobbed forward and back, leaning into the move as he sucked. Rory looked amazing with his shiny red hair and his pouty lips. Watching his dick going in and out of Rory's mouth made his temperature boil. His orgasm came over him in a flash. He shivered and latched on to Rory's shoulders to keep from falling when his knees buckled. With a laugh, Rory shoved him onto the bed.

"Damn, Rory. You killed me." Donner crawled up to the top of the bed. "Now, get up here."

Rory didn't waste any time. He snuggled in next to Donner. His warm body gave him exactly what he needed. He kissed the top of Rory's head. "Thank you, babe."

"For what?"

"Everything."

A banging on the door and screaming kids woke Donner and Rory the next morning. Finley's voice broke when he called to them. "We need to go outside!" He was already hitting puberty.

"It's too bloody early!" He meant both the aging of his kids and getting up.

"Come on!" Alana echoed.

Donner groaned and shook Rory.

"I need coffee first." Rory rubbed his eyes.

"No lie."

They got up, pulled on sweatpants, then opened the door. Finley stood there with Ferdinand resting on his head. "Ferdy wants to come too. Are you ready?" More voice cracking.

Donner couldn't help but smile at their eagerness. They couldn't put off letting the kids outside any longer. "Come on then."

When they got downstairs, Alana handed both him and Rory coffee mugs. *Bless the child.* Both her and Maja wore matching shift-dresses, and their feet were bare.

Rory took his mug. "You look ready."

"I am. We haven't been out in, I don't know, too long. Let's go." She hurried through the living room area, past the fireplace, to the glass doors lining the back wall, tugging Maja the entire way.

Finley trailed after them. Like his fathers, he wore loose sweatpants. He held one hand on his head, keeping Ferdinand from falling off.

Donner sipped his coffee, watching them go. "They're growing up way too fast."

"Can't argue with that." Rory set his mug on a table. "You ready? We're safe out there, right?"

"Yes. Safe as we can be. There are two guards walking the perimeter. We'll have them for a while. At least until things settle."

"You think the war is over then?" Rory asked as he stepped outside.

Donner followed him. "I hope."

With a quick nod, Rory dropped his pants to the ground. The kids' clothes were already lying in a pile on the patio table. "Race you!" He winked then shifted right into a run.

Donner had no clue how he shifted so fast, but he liked the challenge. He set his coffee next to the pile, then he added his clothes and took off after Rory.

They bounced around the kids and locked antlers,

playfully. Donner noticed Finley had a few tines popping through. They weren't fawns anymore, but it was hard to reconcile the fact with the way Finley rolled around on his back with his legs in the air. The mouse ran over his tummy, tickling him.

Soon the other deer from their herd joined them. Rocco flicked his tail as he followed Emma into the field. Emma glanced back at him. She'd become a lovely hind, all graceful and poised. Rocco moved forward, and they rubbed noses. Alana and Maja snorted and shook their heads, ears flopping around. Donner wasn't sure if that was a good or bad reaction to the new couple, but it warmed his heart to see Emma finding new love after the tragedy of losing her mate.

Donner lay in the grass, content to watch the kids play. They jumped and kicked their feet for the joy of it. Rory settled beside him. After a bit, he wanted to talk, so he took his human form and sat cross-legged. He didn't wait to see if Rory would shift. "There will be fall-out from the council decision. I think it was a power play for Brayton. And I haven't heard back from my *special* contact."

Rory rubbed against his shoulder and sniffed the air. In deer form, Rory was huge, almost as big as Donner, and with Donner in human form, Rory towered over him.

"I worry about it. Our family means everything to me."

Rory jerked his head, both antlers slashing the air—he knew. He understood. Then he got up and grunted, lifting his nose high in the air. Someone was coming.

"Kids! Come here. Now." His sharp tone registered with the kids, and they listened, running over and settling into the long grass. It didn't hide them as much as he would have liked, especially with their colors changing from fawn to mature deer.

Rocco stood between the fawns and the edge of the woods, head lowered, protecting them. A moment later, Eryk joined them. He must have already been watching from the house and seen the flash of Emma's tail, triggering an alarm. She stood near the children, flanks quivering. Rory stood beside the other two bucks, head up and appearing very regal.

Rustling through the leaves alerted him to the approach of several animals. Then wolves stepped out of the tree line.

"What do you want? We have armed guards," Donner warned them — or threatened.

"Guns are cheating, you know." Brayton chuckled, stepping out of the woods in human form.

"I thought you were Prichard's crew. But you *are* here unannounced." He was accompanied by five or six wolves, more if there were some hiding in the woods. "So what do you want?"

"Peace." He held his hands up. "Didn't we already establish that?"

"If we did, why are you here?" Donner narrowed his eyes. He no longer trusted their truce.

"I was told you understood politics, Donner. I meant it when I said commerce was my goal. You voted. Now you need to get on board."

"On board? With you?"

"Yes, I have a lot of the same goals as Prichard —"

The deer grunted, huffed, and stomped their hooves.

"Easy." Brayton held his hands up. "We have different means of getting what we want. Mostly."

"What is it you want?"

"Straight to the point. I like that." He took a few steps closer. "We need goods moved, stored. We want to use your property for it. Simple enough."

"What kind of goods."

"The kind the human authorities wouldn't be so pleased about."

It all made sense. This wasn't about the annihilation of

their species. Not for Brayton. And maybe it hadn't been for Prichard, either. The wolves wanted the deer out of the way. Wanted to take their property and use it. How many of those shifters who stood against Brayton were also being used like this?

"No."

"Then, your war will continue. You want more fighting? For your family?" He deliberately moved his gaze to the children, and it pissed Donner off. He did not like his family being threatened.

"I'm not big on ultimatums, Brayton."

Rory snorted again, loudly, drawing Brayton's eyes back to him. "Take some time to think about it." He flicked a piece of grass he'd been fingering to the ground, then turned back the way he'd come. He walked a few paces before stopping. "Not too long," he called over his shoulder. Then he transformed, springing through the air as he sprouted fur and fang. He landed on four wolf paws, then ran off into the trees with his pack following behind.

The adults shifted to human and gathered around him. Rory changed first, and he was pissed. "This is bullshit."

"I know." Donner couldn't argue this time.

"What are you going to do?" Eryk asked.

"You don't get to decide this one alone, Donner," Rory said before Donner had a chance to answer.

Finley shouldered his way through the adults. "Yeah. This is our problem too."

Donner didn't want them around for the conversation. They'd already seen too much. "No. This is for the adults. Why don't you kids grab lunch."

"Because we're not kids, duh," Alana chimed in.

"You saw my antlers. I'm—"

Rory interrupted him with a hand on his shoulder. "Still too young and talking back to your papa."

181

Finley was nearly as tall as Rory and already bulking at the shoulder. "Sorry. I just meant what happens with this affects us all," Finley said.

"Okay, point taken. Let's *all* meet over some lunch." Donner ended the argument. Finley was quiet and rarely spoke out. If he had something to say, it would be worth listening to, and Donner wasn't too proud to learn from the young.

"I think I understand the situation," Finley said after swallowing a bite of sandwich. They'd prepared a quick and easy lunch, mostly using the few leftovers they still had from Mabon. "We've been at war with the wolves. The meeting here the other night was to officially change leadership to someone we could work with, but he turned out to be as bad or worse, if you ask me."

"Sounds like you pretty much got it." Rory handed Finley a napkin. They never stopped being parents.

Donner sat between the kids at the table. "I need to call Martin and tell him what's going on, but we need to decide what to do first."

Alana leaned forward, elbows on the table. "How do we decide?" It was a good question. Perfect to get the conversation going.

"We weigh the pro's and con's." Donner winked at her, and Alana smiled.

Eryk stood up, scraping the legs of the chair. "I can't believe we're even considering this. We don't know what they want to bring here. Drugs? Guns?" He had the smallest child. Lotte had been napping during the other kids' time outside and was now playing quietly upstairs with Isla. Donner wanted Isla's opinion on this, as the oldest deer in the herd. He wouldn't decide without her input.

Finley answered, "If we did let them do this, there would have to be locks. A safe place to store whatever it is away from the house. It's a big property. We're old enough to not mess with it, but I assume we're going to have more children next year." He sounded like he'd been thinking about it.

"I don't know if that will be enough. It's not just the children, Fin. It's the human authorities. If they store illegal contraband of any kind here, and it's raided?" Eryk shook his head. "We'll go to jail. Shifters do not do well in human jails. Worse. Donner will lose this property. We'll be left with no sanctuary."

Rory cleared his throat. "Right, and we can't trust the wolves wouldn't load us up with drugs or whatever then call the authorities themselves. It would end us quicker than Prichard ever could have."

Donner conceded the point. How smart was it to have contracted Prichard's death, after all? He still hadn't heard from the vulture. There might be time to stop it. Not that he wanted Prichard back, but . . .

"I don't like being blackmailed. Held hostage. Ultimately, the long-term risks of losing everything and being under the wolves' control is not worth it. I would rather fight, and there are other ways to do this." Donner looked to Emma and Rocco who hadn't said anything. "Does anyone have a pro to this? Something positive to make me change my mind?"

Emma looked sad. "I don't know. I'm tired of this conflict and hoped a new leader would help, but it only changed their tactics. I want more children." She glanced over at Rocco. "But it was hard bringing Maja into this world." That was true for many reasons. She had been left alone with the death of her mate before they had found her, and she had birthed her child into a chaotic and unsafe world. She must have hoped for a safer place to raise Maja.

"Rocco?" Donner asked.

He shrugged. "I don't have children yet. I've never had an opportunity to mate. Emma is one of the very few hinds I've even known." He winked at her. "Donner, you and Rory have already given me more than I ever believed I'd have." He reached out and took Emma's hand. "I stick with you. No matter what."

Donner expected a snicker or comment from Alana and Maja with Rocco's show of affection, but thankfully, there was none. For once, they were both acting like mature adults. "Girls? Do you have anything to add?"

Maja shook her head, but Alana tilted hers. "What are our tactics? What will we do to fight the wolves? So far we've hidden and let Martin come in with his guns." Alana knew the taboo of guns for shifters. They'd been taught the important things. "Is that how we continue? I don't think it's going to work."

Donner nodded. "Good point. I agree. We have to protect this sanctuary first. We need to do it on our own. We look weak to Brayton and the others by relying on Martin and the council. It's a big property, and a lot of people have been coming and going from the woods. We need to do something about that."

Finley chuckled. "Should have asked me sooner. You need some modern tech, papa."

"Care to elaborate?" Donner asked.

"We need to fence the outer perimeter with an electrified barrier, and we need cameras set up throughout the property with a monitoring station. We'll be able to see what's going on. And have the fence alarmed, in case someone tries to get around it or through it."

Rory bumped his shoulder into Finley's. "Pretty smart, Fin."

Finley blushed and glanced away. He was right about everything. Donner would implement his suggestions immediately. "Easy enough. That's done."

"Okay, better protection, but what about fighting?" Alana

asked, eyes flashing with passion. "We need to fight claw with claw."

Deer didn't have claws. Or fangs. They were generally gentle but not without defense. But this called for more than defense. Alana was right. They needed to find some claws. "Do you have something in mind?"

Alana smiled, obviously happy to be listened to. "I might. I don't know what kind of resources we have. But to me, if we want to show them that we're not backing down, we need to do two things. First, we need more friends on *our* side. And not the council, I mean other shifter groups. Others who have been targeted like we have, who feel alone in this fight."

"You spied on the meeting?" Rory asked, narrowing his eyes.

She side-eyed Maja. "Maybe . . ."

Donner chuckled. They hadn't even suspected, but he was glad they had been listening in. *Those kids are fucking smart.* "What's number two?"

Alana practically beamed then. "We need to attack them where it hurts. Didn't Brayton say something about commerce? We need to know what he's up to. Report *him* to the authorities. Buy property out from under him. Find ways to make them hurt. We need business people to help destroy their financial interests."

"I think you've been watching too many movies, young lady," Emma said.

"Maybe, but she's right." Donner stood up. "And we can move in that direction. I'm sure we can get the right people in place. Is this what we want to do?"

Rory stared up at Donner, holding his gaze with confidence. "I want to hear what Isla has to say."

"So do I. Then we can take a vote."

"Isla is going to agree," Alana said. "We've been talking about this."

"Good to know." Donner only laughed as he went up to talk to the older hind.

Isla got behind fighting the wolves one hundred percent. In fact, she'd been the one to give Alana her phrase *fight claw with claw*. The vote was unanimous. The wolves would not be blackmailing them.

Donner called Martin to fill him in. "We refuse to let another wolf leader bully us into something we don't want," Donner said into his phone. He spun around in his office chair to face the back wall. He'd hung a family portrait there. He and Rory were holding each of their twins. This decision would impact them all. It weighed heavy on his heart, but he had to try to do the right thing — the best thing. The backing of his herd made it a bit easier.

"Donner. I think you should take a little more time to think about all this."

"What? Are you saying we should give in?"

"I told Brayton you would be reasonable."

"Fuck! Damn you, Martin. I thought you understood our side."

"I do. Donner, you have to understand. There's more at stake here. The deer and others are on the brink of extinction. We don't want that. The wolves are powerful. They have the numbers —"

"We'll see."

"It's business. Brayton doesn't give a shit about wiping out others. He only cares about money."

"For the wolves." He got the picture. He might have to withdraw from the council, but not yet. He needed the contacts and the inside information. They needed to be smarter — like his kids — if they wanted to end this mutocide.

"Donner . . ." Martin sighed. "If you're not going to agree to Brayton's request, I'm pulling the security from your property."

Good riddance! He hated having guns on his lands. "I understand."

"Do you?"

"Yes." Donner had already called some of his business contacts to set their plans in motion. He wanted Martin's men gone before they set up security, which he'd scheduled to arrive in the next few hours. They weren't wasting time. "Go ahead and tell them to leave. We're fine."

"This is a mistake. Donner," Martin pleaded. He had helped Donner to set the whole thing up with Brayton. He'd been privy to Brayton's plan. He had lied, or at least left out important aspects of the truth and could no longer be trusted.

Donner turned his chair and looked up to see Rory standing in the doorway. He nodded his approval.

"Thanks for all your help, Martin," Donner said into the phone. "We'll take it from here." He tapped the phone to end the call and noticed a text.

From Vulture.

A sunshine face.

One threat was gone. Donner would have to live with it. He had called for Pritchard's death. The assassination was a cold thing, not like fighting in the field — hooves against fangs. But for his family, Donner would do anything.

He was thankful for his beautiful herd, though. Mabon and the time for feasting was over. They had a lot to do to prepare for the coming months.

Also from Lynn Michaels

Sometimes Demons Whisper: WCPC Paranormal Consultants #1
A Frostbite Christmas: eXtasy Stocking Stuffer
Red Run Rescue: Winter Magic Anthology
Red Run Rut: Spring Fever Anthology
Our Own Story

ABOUT THE LYNN MICHAELS

Lynn Michaels lives and writes in Tampa, Florida where the sun is hot and the Sangria is cold. When she's not writing she's kayaking, hanging with her husband, or reading by the pool. Lynn writes Male/Male romance because she believes everyone deserves a happy ending and the dynamics of male characters can be intriguing, vulnerable, and exciting. She has both contemporary and paranormal titles and has been writing since 2014. Her stories don't follow any set guidelines or ideas, but come from her heart and contain love in many forms.

Lynn's Loonie Bin—Facebook Readers' Group: http://bit.ly/LooneyBinonFacebook

Twitter: https://twitter.com/sljasble

Goodreads: https://www.goodreads.com/author/show/8430620.Lynn_Michaels

eXtasybooks profile: http://www.extasybooks.com/lynn-michaels/

Instagram: https://www.instagram.com/lynnmichaels69/

Say Yes

By

Deja Black

A wolf with trust issues who's afraid of saying yes to wedded bliss and a goblin who wants to put a ring on it. What's a goblin to do?

It's time for the Autumn Feast, a time for celebration, a time for a goblin to finally convince his wolf to marry him. Well, that's what Calyx Akiyama is hoping for, and all the sanctuary with him.

What will it take for Trey Bowden to say yes? How about a war?

DEDICATION

For my little ones, thank you for being willing to share your time so I can tell my tales.

Just like I found my dream, I'll never hesitate to help you discover your own.

Love,
Mommy

Chapter One: Protect Our Own

Calyx stood in the forest with his father, Haru, and his brother, Dimitri, as they scoured the area searching for more signs of the trespassers. For now, they only had shredded earth and bent grasses, clues that those who cared nothing for the property treasured by the sanctuary had been here. There was a chill in the air with autumn approaching, and preparations for the Autumn Feast were in the works.

"When will we have what is required?" Haru asked.

"Soon, Father, the permits, documentation of the action, and all will be in our hands. We've proved the ownership of the land and acquired the witnesses. That should be enough to establish this property belongs to our people. It's the law."

"Waiting for human laws to do what we could do ourselves is interminable," Dimitri growled as he bent at the knee to retrieve a smoldering cigarette from the earth. The only thing in flames in the vicinity of the sanctuary should be incense from the temple. What Dimitri held is his hand was enough to start a forest fire. "While we wait on these actions from human courts that will evidence our ownership of grounds we have protected for centuries, those seeking entry into the sanctuary encroach on our territory and threaten the safety of our people."

Calyx admired his brother, Dimitri, but they had different views. Dimitri was more like their father's first sire, all dark hair and unruly curls, with sparkling green eyes and vicious temperament. Where Dimitri was broad like their father, Calyx was of slimmer build, yet muscular and capable in his own right. His skill lay not in the field of battle like Dimitri's, but in the war of human law as his father had bidden him.

"I would join you in eviscerating them if that were a better choice, Dimitri, but if we are to do this properly, then that paperwork you scoff at is the legal way to ensure our people are safe. The priests have agreed, and we accepted this. They believe in our carrying out their decisions." Calyx spoke calmly, but he was tired of Dimitri's doubts.

"Your brother is correct, my eldest. Times have changed, and the way of the Tengu goblin must change with them." Haru rose then, and the customary gold braid at his back swung with his movement. That was where Calyx' and his father's similarities lay. While Dimitri was all dark power, Calyx was golden, both in hair and body. He was light to Dimitri's dark, a benefit to him when he was in the courtroom. He was not above using his beauty to gain him an extra advantage when needed.

"But . . ." Dimitri argued.

"Even your husband agrees, Dimitri," Haru was quick to add.

Ah, Eric. My brother's human mate. Just seeing the softening of Dimitri's eyes, and the gentle smile that rose when someone mentioned Eric's name, was a blessing to behold. Gone was the hard man Dimitri had been before he fell in love with Eric. Now, the mere thought of Eric could turn the tide from vengeful and angry to warm and calm. Eric was a gift to them all.

Calyx thought back to two nights before, when everyone around them probably heard his brother's cries of *Harder, Eric. More, Eric. Please, Eric.* The sounds of Dimitri's lovemaking had stirred Calyx to seek own his mate, to fuck Trey long and deep, filling him with his seed.

Calyx was grateful to have found the happiness with the mate he'd prayed so many years for, but it wasn't enough. He wanted them to share each other's names, to marry as his brother had married Eric, but each time he'd asked, Trey denied him.

He suspected the reason for the denial was the same that compelled Trey to hesitate to release his wolf. Trey's mother. The pain and fear she'd raised her son with crippled his spirit and his ability to accept love, causing him to erect walls that were formidable to climb, but it was worth it. Trey was worth it. The woman was dead, but her ghost lived on to torture a son she should have protected.

It had taken time for Calyx to draw Trey's wolf out, to free him from the confines of his human self. Now, Trey often ran with him as Calyx took to the skies. They shared in the heat of the chase, and when Calyx snared his wolf and loved him until the night covered them, it was a tremendous moment of passion.

But just as human law was a must to protect their home, Calyx believed their bond required the legal tie as well. There were hindrances without the title of husband or even partner that must be addressed if Calyx wanted to care for Trey in all aspects of their lives. Marriage would give them that, but Trey refused.

"Speaking of mates, Calyx, when will Trey return home?"

"I expect to see him shortly, possibly after I return from the city. He's gone to pick up his cousin, Kindling."

Calyx's father looked up at that. "Ah, so he did decide to bring his family. That's a step forward, isn't it?"

"Yes, it is, actually. He was kept in isolation so long by his mother and separated from his father's people. When his uncle decided to reconnect, Trey was shocked at first. He believed his mother's rants that he was unwanted, that she was the only one who loved him."

Trey's mother was a wolf just as her mate was, but humans had killed her mate, and she'd turned her back on their people. It had taken Calyx bringing Trey to a place where his wolf could run free to dismantle the fear that kept both his mate and his wolf prisoner.

"That's no way to live," Dimitri said as he opened his wings fanning the air about them. "Hmm. There were at least six of them, and they carried weapons." He breathed deep. "Guns. An accelerant. We'll have to increase our guard tonight."

Haru nodded. "I'll inform the priest. We should also move the elderly and children to safety. Higher ground?"

"Yes. After? Perhaps a spell?" Dimitri questioned.

"No, not now. The magic of the earth is only called forth when all else fails, especially with the approach of the Autumn Feast. It is the time for rest, for conserving energy. There are other options," Haru explained.

"We could kill them all. I vote for that one." Dimitri's smile was all sharp teeth and fang.

Haru laughed when Calyx shook his head. "We might begin there, my son, but where will it end? Let's try this the legal way first. At least we'll know we attempted all else before a drop of blood spills."

Dimitri brought his wings in close to his body and turned to their father, nodding. "But if it doesn't work . . ."

"Then we will do what's necessary to protect our own," Calyx agreed.

Dimitri nodded, and the three of them turned toward home.

CHAPTER TWO: OVER THE HILLS

Trey drove the truck Calyx had insisted he own along the treacherous road leading to the mountain top. He would have argued more to keep his beater car if his mate wasn't correct about the condition of the almost fifteen-year-old vehicle. He'd heard the words *not safe* and *rust bucket* often enough that he'd surrendered to remove the words from Calyx's vocabulary. It was a concession he'd given, another piece of his control. Still, it was better than answering yes to a question Calyx refused to stop asking.

Marriage. Calyx wanted to marry him, for the two of them to share the same last name as humans did, as Calyx's brother and his human mate had done.

Why the binding contract?

What signed document could hold up to the sheer power of a mated pair? But, no! For months, Calyx had waged a crusade against Trey and his denial of wedded bliss.

Marriage.

Permanence.

Abandonment.

After all, was marriage not one of the things his mother had warned him of? Trey remembered promising never to enter a bond easy to get into but arduous to leave.

Trey's father made his mother promises of a life together forever as husband and wife, of moonlit nights where they would run as wolves.

His father made promises of love.

The first promise he'd broken was his faithfulness. Instead

of spending those nights with Trey's mother, he'd traveled to the embrace of another, a human woman whose body he favored more than the mate who'd given all of herself. His mother gave all the tenderness she never shared with her son to a husband who failed to value it. It was his father's misfortune the human he'd chosen had been the daughter of a hunter. That hunter felt no remorse in ridding the world of a monster, one who'd defiled his offspring.

Never mind the *monster* had a wife and a child.

His father was dead, but his legacy lived on in his mother's fears.

Never change.

Never release your wolf.

Never marry.

Trey had already broken the first two promises, and his mate was trying for a triple play.

And Calyx wasn't alone in his campaign. He had enlisted the help of his father, Haru, who had not married a mate of his own but saw nothing wrong with extolling its virtues for his sons. And not just Haru, but it seemed the entire community had joined the cause.

He'd been asked when the date would occur, been offered places for the ceremony, and reminded of suitable times by nearly every member of the sanctuary.

Every day.

It was driving him crazy. At night when Calyx drove into his body, entwining their souls together once more, he couldn't get the fucking questions out of his head.

When Calyx lapped at his skin murmuring tender words, Trey knew what the man wanted.

"Are we getting closer?" Kindling asked.

Trey had been trapped in his thoughts and recognized the thread of impatience lacing his cousin's words.

The same tone laced his mate's words enough these days as the Autumn Feast drew nearer.

"Soon," Trey muttered, grunting as they hit another bump along the way, this one nearly making him rise off the seat.

"Why can't we park this monster truck and wolf out? We take off, run, and enter this sanctuary you speak of so lovingly. We could come back for the vehicle in the morning."

"Our clothes." Trey sighed, trying for patience. It was a necessity when dealing with Kindling, whose energy was not for the weak. They had time before they had to park his *monster truck,* as Kindling called it. Then they could grab their bags and walk into the veil.

"Aw, come on! Like these people would be shocked to see a few dangly parts." Kindling crossed his slim arms in an imitation of a two-year-old.

From what Trey had learned of his free-spirited cousin, he had no hesitation in showing his *dangly parts*. When Trey had arrived to pick him up from his apartment, Kindling had been stark naked, his brown skin glistening with water and foam from a shower. Kindling had opened the door without hesitation, his amber eyes shiny with recognition.

Trey had had no idea what meeting Kindling would be like after all those years of absence. They'd been children, he older than Kindling by at least six years, or was it more? Hell, Kindling had been a pup, nothing like the creature that bounced in the seat next to him, a Jack-in-the-box waiting to pop out of an open door and hit the grass running.

His mother hadn't reached out to their pack after his father died, choosing to be a recluse instead. She didn't trust his father's brother, his family, or his pack. After all, she'd accepted them into her life, married their brother, only to be abandoned by him with a young child to raise.

She'd wanted no part of them. She'd taken her son and returned to her people, shamed and broken, staying long enough to get on her feet and then deserting them as well.

Alone.

Always alone.

It had only been the two of them.

"I mean, really? Who would care? All this land? Let's go for it," Kindling persisted.

Trey shook his head. He would be lying to himself if he didn't admit how much he envied the way Kindling accepted his wolf. He was mercury on two legs the way he flowed and danced around any obstacle. Trey liked him and was pleased Calyx had suggested reconnecting with his family, with his people.

Trey had reached out, and his uncle had been pleased to hear from him. He'd known about Trey and his mother, where they'd lived, and that Trey had moved away. He'd kept watch as much as he could, considering his mother's hatred of them. But Trey was his brother's son, and he'd hoped they could repair the divide someday.

When Uncle Lore had suggested they start with Trey and Kindling spending time together, it was Calyx who proposed bringing him to the sanctuary. Trey knew what his mate was thinking. The more wolves Trey surrounded himself with, the more comfortable he would become with his beast. They would see.

"We're going to wait until we're close enough. Then, maybe?"

Kindling seemed to vibrate with those words. "All right! So tell me about this place. You know I'm still trying to decide where my feet will take me, that I'm sort of in transition right now with my school closing. Even though the district promises we'll have a job, I'm not so sure I want to stay in Tennessee, keep teaching there. I'm glad you came along, even if my dad was the one who suggested it."

Yeah, that had been Lore's motivation when he'd told Trey, "Kindling needs some direction. He's too much of a free spirit, and his mother is worried."

Trey read the subtext there. Lore was concerned. Trey finding his mate was enough for his uncle to pray their lost lamb would imprint on his older cousin and perhaps find his own.

Trey didn't know about Kindling finding a mate, but having his company for the last couple of hours had been nice, if never quiet.

Family. He could feel the way their wolves were sniffing each other out beneath the surface, recognizing their connection. Trey's shivered in excitement with the possibility of companionship. His wolf was restless, and his skin felt like it was crawling with ants.

"There are mountains and lakes and space to run. The goblins, my mate included, act as guardians for the sanctuary, and are protective when it comes to the people there."

"Goblins. It's still crazy to me that you, a wolf, are mated to a goblin. But hey! Love is love, right? What are the humans like there? They already have goblins. They know you're a wolf. Does it freak them out at all?" Kindling growled, holding his hands up in the parody of a monster ready to attack. "Come here, human. I will eat you."

"No, Kindling. They're not worried. And if you tried that, you'd be surprised." The humans there were not without protection. The earth magic kept them safe, the ancient elders well trained in wielding its power. It was a sort of symbiotic relationship.

Kindling laughed, obviously not the least frightened. "Okay, so do they live in houses, in the trees, how's that work?"

"There are houses, a temple, and even a few of those tree houses you laugh about. Cabins, too. The most important thing for them is they're together. There are families, and with the families, children. It's a village."

"How do they sustain themselves?"

"The earth provides." Trey indicated the changing

panorama of the trees and vegetation. The colors of gold, red, orange, and green were brilliant against the skyline. "The sanctuary is home to minerals not found around the world, which they trade under the name of different companies to shield their identities. They also create crafts and art sold in galleries and shops at the mountain base."

"The stores we passed on the way up here?"

"Yes."

Kindling nodded. "I remember seeing a few of the pieces. Beautiful. Unique. I hope to purchase a few myself." His words were wistful, and Trey wondered not for the first time what it was Kindling needed. There were these crazy bursts of energy from the man, then these spaces of quiet that were worrisome.

"Kindling? What's going on?"

"Nothing. Forget it." Kindling murmured. "It sounds like someplace wonderful to be, like a home. And, you know, I've been looking for that."

Trey heard the sadness in Kindling's voice and wanted to help. The sanctuary *was* home for him, a place where he could be himself. He'd found his place there at Calyx's side as a teacher, a guide for the youth, because even in a community so insular, there were still troubled youth needing someone to trust. Trey was vital, a part of something. Perhaps being vital was what Kindling was looking for, too.

"What did you do again?" he asked.

"I was a counselor, and then I wasn't. Budget cuts, you know."

"Yeah, that's happening more and more." His kids could benefit from a counselor, someone who was an outsider able to listen to their needs objectively.

"So, here I am—money in the bank, two intrusive parents, and a vacation in the mountains. And you, when are you and Calyx tying the knot? Knot! Ha!" Kindling's laugh was catchy even if the topic was one Trey had been trying to avoid.

"We're not."

"You're not?" A snicker, then Kindling sobered. "Really?"

"Look, I don't want to talk about it."

"Okay, no problem." Kindling looked out the window, and the tense quiet lasted about five seconds before his cousin shot off another question. "What's the Autumn Feast for?"

Trey considered how to explain the sanctuary's celebration of the Autumn Feast as he drove along the path approaching the drop-off point. He could feel the veil's presence and prepared to park. He pulled the truck between the trees, which would act as a curtain, hiding the vehicle within its shadows.

Once it was safely hidden away, Trey pushed the driver's door open and hopped down and waited until Kindling followed suit. He almost reached out to help the smaller man before he thought better of it.

Kindling smiled at him, knowingly. "Yeah, we weren't all blessed with the strength and height of the alphas, but I make up for it in my sexual prowess." He winked.

Trey snorted, and Kindling laughed.

"So, the Autumn Feast is a celebration of the earth's rest, a turning-over before sleep arrives in the form of winter. It's the oranges and reds, the flames of the land."

"Will there be sex?" Kindling asked as he tugged a duffel bag from the back and a brown leather backpack.

Trey coughed. "Not an orgy, Kindling. It's a celebration."

"Sex is a celebration," Kindling argued. "What?" He shrugged when Trey glared at him. "They're pagans, right? Goes hand-in-hand with sex."

"For one thing, that's not true, and I think you know this." Trey had learned Kindling liked to push buttons. He was a minx, all slim and graceful with a wiry musculature beneath. He sported a head of loose curls that caught the light as they traveled. He was a pretty man, one Trey was certain had his pick of dates, male or female. He had yet to figure out which Kindling preferred, if there was a preference at all.

"Yeah, just testing you. It's what I do. Haven't seen you in forever. Now we're visiting your cult in the mountains that's a group of ancient people guarded by goblins. Makes me a little weirded out, but okay. Sorry." He dragged on the backpack and picked up the duffel, then signaled he was ready. "So reds, yellows, and the earth takes a dirt nap. What else?"

"It's an Asian harvest festival," Trey explained as they walked toward the veil. "A time for family and friends to come together when the moon is at its brightest and roundest."

"So, the party is at night and includes the moon. Sounds perfect for us four-legged beasts, too."

Trey smiled. "It is. Everyone in the sanctuary celebrates — the people, the elders, goblins, and the wolves, or in my case, wolf."

"Well, now it can be wolves."

That was true, until Kindling took off. This wasn't a permanent stay. Kindling was there to visit for a month or two, time enough for him to get his head together and then return to the city. That was it.

Trey said nothing.

"Okay, not awkward at all. So, celebration. Is it like Thanksgiving, then? Will there be a turkey?"

"No, but there will be mooncakes."

Kindling nodded. "Cakes."

"Yes, and praying for babies, for marriages, beauty, longevity, and good futures. For hope in the coming winter."

"Huh. Marriage, you say?"

Trey huffed. They were nearing the veil. He could feel the brush of energy over his skin grow stronger as the sanctuary recognized him.

"Look, Trey. I know something is happening in your head

involving your commitment phobia, but if the man makes you as happy as you look when you talk about him, why not just go ahead and take the plunge?"

Trey's face grew warm, and his smile bloomed before he could stop it. He had to remind himself it was fine to be happy, that there was nothing to be guilty about. He had someone who loved him. Instead of hiding it, he should shout it to the heavens, but sometimes he remembered his mother as she cried alone at night, her sobs behind her bedroom door and he worried.

For him, Calyx was the sun. Trey's light had found him, and all he wanted to do was drink it in.

Each day was a step closer for them. His wolf recognized Calyx's goblin, enticed him in the wood when they gave chase.

He was happy. Gods, he was, and he never wanted to let it go.

"See. That right there, that glowy thing you're doing with your face. That's why."

Trey laughed, feeling ten times lighter with the thought of seeing his mate soon.

"Come on, you. Let's go."

Balancing the rest of their items, Trey stepped forward. Taking a deep breath, he waited until the trees slowly bent their thick limbs toward him, the foliage offering a welcoming caress.

CHAPTER THREE: I'LL SHOW YOU MINE

"Here is the sanctuary." It had been an extraordinary moment the first time Trey entered the veil nearly four
years ago. To a passerby, this was just a cluster of trees. To the
people who lived here and the goblins guarding them and
their secrets, it was a huge, bustling village with people strid-
ing to and fro along paths that led to different dwellings in
the center where goods were made. Birds flew in arcs in the
sky, silent outside of the sanctuary, but their songs were beautiful here.

The temple stood back off the path, and Trey could make
out the goblins standing before it as well as the ones standing
at the towers, their wings ready to take flight should there be
cause.

There was life here, a school in the distance, a whole world
within the veil. Trey would take Kindling to where he and
Calyx often played, Trey's paws pounding the earth and Calyx speeding after him, his wings beating the air. Trey's dick
grew hard and eager with the memory.

Kindling suddenly took a deep breath, and then the little
imp looked at him with a sly grin.

"Not. A. Word."

"I wasn't going there — this time. Besides, I'd rather take all
of this in. Why do they even need to leave here? The only
thing missing is a mall and a Starbucks."

Trey laughed. "We have a coffee shop here, and what it
serves, Starbucks can't find. And a mall? Well, there's a delivery service. We're not without technology. There are

computers in a library where they are monitored regularly. Young ones, you know." There were benefits to technology, but there were detriments, too.

"Amazing"

It was.

"Trey," called a voice Trey recognized. He waited as the leader of the goblins moved toward him, his large body cutting a path through those bustling around him.

Though Haru wasn't in goblin form, Trey could envision the colossal black leathery wing appendages spread wide beyond his frame, casting the world behind him in shadow.

"Haru, this is my cousin, Kindling, the one I mentioned visiting."

Green eyes, the color of the forest, turned toward Kindling, and Haru nodded with a gentle smile. "Welcome, young one, to our sanctuary. I'm glad you're here. Perhaps my son's mate" — Haru focused on Trey — "and future husband will not be a lone wolf for a while." He laughed warmly.

Trey shook his head. "I think he plans —" Trey coughed when Kindling elbowed him in the ribs, moving him out of the way and planting himself before Haru, who dwarfed him.

Haru was a wide redwood and Kindling a twig.

"To stay forever." Kindling finished. "Is that an option? I love what I've seen so far." There was a rough growl to Kindling's voice as he gracefully eased forward with each word until his body aligned against Haru's.

Haru stepped back in surprise, only for Kindling to swiftly remove the distance gained. Trey almost felt sorry for his mate's father. Almost.

"Forever?" Haru questioned while again trying to place some space between him and Kindling.

"Yes. And I didn't come just to see my cousin. I came to see the world he's found, his home, and explore, as my father called it. I'd hate to take all Trey's time I'm sure he'd rather spend with his mate." Kindling placed a finger against his lips as if in thought, and Trey snorted as Haru's eyes followed the movement. "Maybe you could help with that? You know, show me around?" Kindling gracefully pointed out the area.

Trey smelled it then, the perfume of sexual heat coming off Kindling's body, and registered a similar response from Haru, including both desire and trepidation. It was unusual, and unlike the charismatic, fatherly warrior Trey knew.

Kindling wasn't holding back, though. If anything, Haru's scent must have been a siren call to his cousin, because Trey saw the moment Kindling's teeth lost their human appearance and shifted into fangs.

"A run sounds great," Trey rushed out. "In fact, Kindling, let's go on one right now."

"No," Kindling argued. "I want to stay here." He licked his bottom lip hungrily, ensnaring Haru further in his trap.

Can't wait to tell Calyx about this. Trey dragged his cousin away from Haru Akiyama, High Lord of the Tengu Goblins.

"I wasn't going to hurt him," Kindling protested.

"No? You looked like you wanted him to mount you for all in the sanctuary to see."

"Yes, that would have been lovely. Your sanctuary into that type of thing? I wouldn't have minded."

"No, of course, you wouldn't."

"Don't be crass. And, even better? Me mounting him, my swollen cock between those tight cheeks of his. Did you see that ass? He could crack walnuts with that thing."

Trey groaned. He had to get the man to the glen . . . now.

Kindling had been given his own place to stay because, and Trey hated to admit it, he didn't feel like he'd fully claimed Calyx yet. Until that happened, he couldn't trust he wouldn't eviscerate any perceived challenger for his mate's affections.

Hopefully, his cousin wouldn't embarrass him by trying to drag Haru to his den to do things Haru might want but seemed apprehensive to accept.

Calyx and Trey's home was very similar to where Kindling would be staying, including a fireplace, two floors, and three bedrooms. Their ceilings were higher, with massive windows leading to balconies where Calyx could walk fully shifted and fly from the edge if necessary.

A library existed on the second floor of each house, but Kindling's was empty where Calyx and Trey's overflowed with law books, journals, texts, and their favorite authors, some they shared and some they didn't. Calyx liked mysteries, while Trey's taste was more non-fiction and romance, which surprised his mate.

Both homes had spacious kitchens. Calyx made great use of theirs, with occasional help from Trey. He didn't know if Kindling cooked, but after a brief inspection of the home, his cousin immediately asked if there was a chance for delivery.

Trey chuckled and informed him that while he couldn't expect a pizza chain or use a delivery service app, there were eateries willing to cater to his needs.

With that covered, they ventured out only to find Dimitri standing at the door as if he'd been listening the entire time.

Trey sighed. To Dimitri, Kindling was an outsider, and the way his mate's brother watched his cousin raised Trey's hackles.

"We've been over this, Dimitri. He's staying."

"While I still disagree, your cousin's presence is not my current concern." Dimitri sniffed the air and glared at Kindling, studying him like a bug under a magnifying glass. "You smell like my father," he growled.

"Well," Trey interjected, "the two of them did meet, and it was . . . interesting."

"Was it?" Dimitri inhaled again and raised an eyebrow in question.

"Oh, yes. Very." Kindling growled. "I'm hoping for a

repeat later with me all over him."

Dimitri's gaped in surprise.

"Yes, Kindling is open—"

"Like a book." Kindling laughed.

Trey cleared his throat. "So, the warning, or the reason you're here and not with your husband or prowling the grounds?"

"There have been signs of outsiders along the perimeter. Trespassers."

"Is that even possible?" Trey questioned. Not only was the security of the sanctuary above reproach, but Calyx had also filed an action to ensure development companies were kept away. Was this a real worry, or was Dimitri paranoid?

"If they've had help, which I suspect, it is possible. Remember there are those who are against the elders, the keepers of the earth's magic here. For years, they have searched, and there are times when we've had to battle against them. It has been a long time, but that doesn't remove the possibility.

"We found evidence of the threat, and Calyx has gone to the city to report our findings. This should not have happened. There are signs posted, notices. I have disagreed with this, as it only tells others there are things here worth noticing."

It was an argument the brothers often had. Dimitri was from a time when they annihilated the enemy. Calyx was born to a time where they respected the law, knew there were rules to be followed. Blood and death were not the first choices, no matter what Dimitri believed.

"Calyx is trying, Dimitri."

"Trying, yes. Succeeding is yet to be seen. I will wait until we are no longer able. Then, we will fight. I have only come to ask if you planned to go for a run. I would insist you remain in your home, but I know you will only say no. If you would like, I can keep watch from the air, one of my guards or me."

Trey smiled, knowing Dimitri cared about him. After he had fallen in love with a human—after nearly losing him because he thought a man missing a leg was somehow lesser—he'd changed. This Dimitri was warmer, kinder, and even laughed out loud, especially if Eric was with him.

Trey cared for Dimitri, too. The man only wanted the people under his watch to be safe, and Trey knew Dimitri would die to protect those he loved. It had been a rocky start for the two of them, Dimitri trusting no one and Trey questioning his place in the sanctuary and his mate's family. When Eric came along, Dimitri softened, and Trey had come to love him like a brother.

And now, Dimitri wanted to protect him.

"Thanks, Dimitri, no guard necessary," Trey said.

Dimitri harrumphed.

"Truly."

"The pretty man's only asking to be polite, Trey," Kindling said, interrupting the exchange.

"He's taken, Kindling."

"Not interested, Trey. My dance card is full, and I'm simply admiring the genetics."

Dimitri snorted. "Your cousin is right. This was to be polite. Do not try to elude the guard, Trey."

Trey shook his head.

Later, when he found himself coughing up blood as his body healed from a gunshot wound, he remembered questioning Dimitri. The man had been right after all.

CHAPTER FOUR: CLOSER THAN CLOSE

Calyx wondered what his next approach should be to convince Trey to say *yes* to wedded bliss. Maybe he should just leave it alone, wait. Was it life or death for Trey to take his name or for Calyx to take Trey's? No. But there was just something within Calyx burning for the right to call Trey his husband.

Even Dimitri had married, shocking everyone who knew him. He had fallen in love with Eric—a human impaired in body only—claimed him, and brought him home. Eric had fallen into life at the sanctuary easily. His military experience proved vital, and his role supported Dimitri's perfectly.

Don't Trey and I have that?

Calyx protected the sanctuary through his knowledge of the law. His mind was a steel trap, one that memorized every case available to help his people.

Trey was a teacher. He aided in the transition of the young ones to the world beyond the veil. He taught them what they needed, had even begun training others to help.

They made a good team as they worked to move the people and his goblin brethren forward.

Why can't we be a team that shares the same name, wear rings marking us as more than mates while on the sanctuary grounds but as belonging to each other wherever we travel in the world?

Sure, the laws were different from state to state and even from country to country, but there were limits to what Calyx could do for Trey without the title of husband and partner.

He wanted to protect his mate no matter what. To Calyx,

that meant saying *I do*.

He craved it selfishly for himself as well. Seeing what Dimitri had made Calyx want it more. He only had to fight Trey's fears and his mate's dead mother's tainting of what marriage could be.

He sighed as he pulled the car into the notch beside Trey's truck. It had been a battle to get his mate to accept a new vehicle, one held together with more than duct tape and a prayer. It was one of their first hurdles, one of the hardest, and a prelude of things to come.

He opened the car door and felt a crushing blow to his soul. It was an inferno in the pit of his stomach, warning signals tearing up and down his body.

Calyx hefted his wings and took to the air in search of his mate. He could hear the broken howl of his mate's wolf, the disbelief he would be harmed, suffer in a place where he was supposed to be safe.

Their home.

Calyx wanted to roar his anger, destroy those who had injured his mate. Trey was in pain, and Calyx had been absent, trying to fight the right way, the just way. And what had that done? Allowed Trey to be hurt.

He flew past tall trees, swiftly skirting around them as he sought their home. The indigo blue stone appeared, the color they'd finally chosen, Trey's favorite. Trey hadn't wanted to make the decision, too afraid of committing to anything, to submit to the feelings they both shared. With time, Trey relaxed, no longer ready to run at the first chance. Trey chose pictures for the living room, picked up pottery for the library, and even prepared a few meals. Inedible meals, but it was a start.

And someone damaged that. How far would this set us back?

Calyx would kill them and fuck the law.

He landed near their home, his wings settling at his back. He shifted as he neared the doorway, his beak changing into a nose and forming lips for a mouth no longer bearing sharp teeth and fangs. His body lost its massive size, and his claws retracted.

All about him the sanctuary was in chaos, preparing for war. Dimitri's guards were dressed in their armor, wings at the ready. His brother was not present, no doubt his first thought to protect and defend. He would already be in the skies, his eyes peeled for more trouble.

Calyx could hear the human men, women, and children readying themselves as well. Those who were vulnerable would be secured. Typically, the men went with them, and the elders were kept in the temple, where they would remain unless earth magic was necessary. Now, everyone who was able would fight.

There was a time long ago when those who followed the Meiji, ancients who remained determined to rid the world of the Shugenja, reigned freely. For centuries, the Tengu had protected the Shugenja, curators of the mountains, caretakers of the earth magic. And for just as long, the Meiji sought to eradicate them.

Is there no room for peace? Why did there have to be one way to believe, one way to worship? Why destroy people who only sought to do good in the world?

But power and the desire to use it ran rampant. The Meiji had connections globally, those willing to pay significantly for the magic kept by the Shugenja.

And now his mate had been hurt, his brother and his guards off to fight more than a supposed company bent on development, but a faction determined to eradicate the sanctuary and those who protected it. Calyx had learned the parent company of the business, revealed the monopoly behind it. It was included in the action, something that was supposed to help them, but it hadn't been enough.

Calyx knew Eric led the soldiers he'd been training, the humans who'd been craving usefulness for years. They followed

Eric and listened to his command. They refused to be sheltered, hidden away any longer with those who were vulnerable and the young. They wanted to fight and found their leader in a man who had given up battle because he no longer thought himself whole.

Here, Eric had found his purpose. And Dimitri was better, stronger for his mate's presence. He found balance. And if either of them was harmed, ended up in a hospital somewhere, neither would be barred from seeing their mate.

Because they were married.

This was all too close a call for him.

Calyx entered his home, the doors vanishing before him. When he burst into their bedroom, Trey opened his arms, and Calyx went to him, falling to his knees beside the bed. His mate was alive, safe, his body healing as Calyx scanned him for injury. Their bond had done that. As a shifter, his mate could heal quickly, but being the mate of a Tengu goblin would expedite the process. They weren't impervious to death, though, neither of them. He could have lost him.

"My love," Calyx whispered.

"I'm fine, Calyx. A little battered, which should disappear soon, but I'm here." Trey reached up and bent his fingers to trail along Calyx's cheek, to smooth away the lines of worry there.

"What happened? Tell me."

"I took Kindling for a run with me."

Kindling.

He turned to where Trey was looking and saw the man sitting in one of the large leather chairs they kept in their bedroom, his eyes still wide with shock. The smile he wore was shaky, but they were both alive. That was all that mattered.

Calyx nodded and turned back to Trey. "Continue."

"Well, Dimitri warned us to be careful, but we were still close enough to the sanctuary we should have been fine when we scented a rabbit. We gave chase."

Calyx sighed. While grateful his mate no longer feared his wolf, he needed to remain vigilant. He was a wolf introduced to the wild after being contained for so long. There were dangers, even near the sanctuary.

"The guard?"

"Flew above us as you have, but even he was not prepared for the men with guns who only saw wolves when we left the safety of the sanctuary."

"Fucking hells, Trey. You're not supposed to leave the boundary."

"I know, Calyx, but it happened before I'd even realized it. And there were too many of them, prepared for more than just a trip to the mountains. They were heavily armed and had others with them."

His father entered the room, a cup of tea in his hand that he gave to Trey who looked at him, a grimace on his face.

"Drink it, my son. It will make the pain disappear faster. Your body is mostly healed, but this will help."

"But . . ."

Calyx growled, "Trey."

Trey shook his head and took a sip.

"How did you get back?"

Trey nodded toward the corner where Kindling huddled. "He shifted, picked me up, and carried me. He brought me back here and sounded the alarm for the others."

Calyx smiled at the man. "Thank you, Kindling. I am grateful to you for caring for Trey, and for warning our people."

Kindling shrugged, uncomfortable with the praise, it seemed. "Anyone would have done it."

"No, not anyone. You did. And that matters greatly to me."

"And to me," Haru said.

There was a trace of heat in his father's voice Calyx had never heard before. He glanced from his father to Kindling, but when Trey coughed, he forgot them immediately, his attention drawn to his mate.

"He did well. Now kiss me," Trey whispered.

Calyx sighed into the kiss, the beating of his heart settling to a more natural rhythm now that the terror of his mate in danger dissipated. The kiss was gentle at first, but then Trey nipped his lips and drank from him, making his goblin rise to the surface. His cock hardened, and his fangs dropped. Calyx had to hold back before he found himself on top of his mate, trying to sink into his body as he sought the closeness, the assurance he was indeed as fine as he said.

"I need to go and fight alongside with Dimitri," Calyx insisted.

"No, my son, you do not. Your part in this is different, has always been. Dimitri is for battle. You will stay here and take care of your mate. I will see that Dimitri and his guards are ready and secure the temple," his father demanded.

"I can fight." He'd had the same training, knew how to hold a weapon, and use the power of the wind. He was not incapable.

"Of that, I have no doubt," Haru consoled, "but you each have your roles to play. We have moved to one your brother and his mate must fulfill."

"What if he needs more? What if there are not enough?" Calyx argued.

"Then you will provide that. Right now, our people take to the air to scourge the sanctuary of the intruders. They will decimate them, as is our right. They chose to enter our lands. They chose the outcome."

"They're armed. We know this."

"And they know we have people here, people they've endangered. I have no doubt they are connected to the Meiji, as you discovered. The court will not be pleased with this violation of the law." He smiled evilly. "They even shot one of our dogs. Humans love their pets. It is the story you will weave, should it become necessary."

Kindling snickered, and Haru smiled softly at him. "Thank you, Kindling, for what you did today. You are stronger than you look."

And there it was again, that heat Calyx heard. *What is going on between Father and Trey's cousin?*

Kindling looked up at Haru, challenging. "So, will my act of heroism be rewarded?"

Haru walked to him as if drawn by the man. Bending, he kissed him softly on the cheek.

Kindling sighed and reached up to touch the cheek Haru's lips had grazed, and Calyx felt the temperature in the room rise.

"Thank you, Kindling. Now, let us leave these two to talk. You may come with me."

"Come, you say?" Kindling quipped.

"Kindling," Haru warned.

Kindling laughed as they left the room, going down the stairs and out of the home. Calyx heard them, but he had eyes only for one person, one wayward man he needed like air to breathe.

Trey's hungry gaze stared. "I want you."

"Trey?" Calyx questioned, struggling against the needs of his inner beast. No matter how fast his mate's healing was, it couldn't be right to take him, to flip him over and find his way home inside his body. He ground his teeth and held himself back.

"No, Calyx. I need you, need you to take me, love me."

"I already love you, Trey. And need? My life would cease were you ever to leave me behind. My heart beats for you." That wasn't the only thing beating, though. Right then, his dick wanted to show his mate just how much he was loved. Calyx drew his hands into fists before his claws made a reappearance.

Trey sighed, then pulled the cover from his beautiful, long body, all of him displayed before Calyx. Amber eyes watched him as Trey wrapped one hand around his dick and tugged it, bringing a pearly drop to the red tip.

Calyx was losing his grip on the scrap of sanity left to him. His mate had been injured, and he hadn't been there to protect him—someone else had stepped in. While Calyx was more than grateful to Kindling, he was ravenous for Trey, the overwhelming desire to scent him, own him, more than he could bear.

Trey looked up at him again, then, drawing his tongue along his teeth, he took a finger and placed it between lips Calyx hungered to taste again. He sucked on the digit and reached beneath himself, grunting when he inserted it into his hole.

"Fuck, Trey."

"That's what I'm trying to get you to do, Calyx. You know you want to. The way you're looking at me and that leviathan dick of yours pleading for entry? Mmm." Trey moaned, and Calyx growled when another finger joined the last.

His willpower was non-existent where Trey was concerned. Entranced by the sight of his mate working his body in preparation for him, Calyx knelt on the bed and crawled up the length of his lover. He trailed gentle kisses along the disappearing bruises, inhaled Trey's scent as he savored his flesh. He bent his head when he arrived at his destination and opened his mouth, taking Trey's heavy member down his throat and sucking deep.

Trey's scream as Calyx ran his claws along his skin was the pot at the end of the rainbow, the Holy Grail. He drew his fangs along Trey's dick, reveling in the sounds his mate made.

"Want you," he growled while placing both hands beneath Trey's thighs, pressing them back until Trey's hole was revealed. "Need you," he rumbled as he dragged his mate to him.

"Please, Calyx," Trey begged and shouted loud enough for the entire sanctuary to hear as Calyx slammed into him, shoving himself deep into his mate's body. "Oh, yes. Oh, yes. Yes, Calyx!"

Trey's repeated cries of Calyx's name made him thrust even deeper, completely one with the man, the wolf he loved.

"Trey, never leave me."

"Never, Calyx. I would never leave you."

Tears ran down Calyx's cheeks as he fucked his mate, owning his ass, trying to feel the beat of his heart on the end of his dick. Trey was hurt, had been shot. He could have been killed.

Bending over his mate, Calyx admired Trey's open mouth as he shouted his pleasure, watched his hands reach for the headboard, trying to stop himself from going through the wall as Calyx fucked his way into his soul.

"My heart, Trey. You are my heart. Please, Trey." Calyx begged and stretched Trey wider until he could feel his balls slapping hard against his mate's fiery ass.

"Whatever you need, whatever you want."

"Please, Trey." Calyx had no idea what he wanted, what he hoped as the sobs tore out of him, as the fear of what could have happened raced through him. He fell on top of Trey then, his tears dropping on Trey's skin, his heart trying to rip itself out of his body.

"Calyx, oh Gods, Calyx. So sorry, baby. So sorry. I'm so sorry."

Calyx released one of Trey's thighs and used an arm to rid himself of the wetness. "You can't do this to me, can't love me, then . . . Fuck." Calyx had never wanted anything for himself. He was a goblin. He knew his place, his role in the sanctuary. He'd gone to school, having no idea he would meet this man, that his heart would beat for the first time when they met . . . when he claimed Trey as his.

Then to have almost lost him.

He kissed Trey, swallowing his tongue, drinking him in. He sighed when Trey touched his cheeks, gently wiped away the tears that still fell.

"I love you, Calyx. I do."

Calyx nodded, too overwhelmed to speak. He kissed Trey again before picking his mate up, turning him over, and slamming into him from behind. He draped himself over Trey's back and fucked him ruthlessly, celebrating Trey's moans before he wrapped his arms underneath him and pulled him back against him so he could drill himself in further.

He reached low to take Trey's bobbing dick in his hand, tugging it in sync with his thrusts, riding Trey's pleasure when he exploded. It was magical, the way his seed spilled over Calyx's fingers, the taste blissful on his tongue.

"Calyx?" Trey questioned.

He heard the worry in Trey's words, the uncertainty.

Calyx wouldn't allow his own bliss, though, not until he'd heard the words he craved as much as life itself. He continued fucking Trey, his mate's greedy hole swallowing his aching dick, bringing him closer to the abyss.

"Say it. Please, Trey."

"Oh, Calyx, my baby. Make me yours, again."

Calyx struck then, sank his fangs deep into Trey's waiting neck as he filled Trey's ass with his seed. It was so marvelous, this gift his mate gave to him, his submission, his sacrifice, and the taste of his seed combined with that of his blood was an ambrosia Calyx craved.

"I love you, Calyx. I do. So much," Trey cried as he fell limply into their bed.

Calyx wrapped himself around Trey as he continued pumping inside Trey's body, his breathing returning to normal and the tremors leaving him sated.

"And I, you," he whispered.

They couldn't stay too long. No matter what his father said, they had to help. War had come to the sanctuary, and everyone had a role to play.

"Soon, okay?" Trey murmured.

Calyx burrowed his face into the curve of his mate's neck and smiled.

Soon. He could wait.

CHAPTER FIVE: READY OR NOT

Eric made sure his men were ready, reminding them to be alert and to be prepared to use the weaponry sanctioned by the elders. All were eager to fight and had come a long way since Eric first arrived. For too long, the people of the sanctuary had been accustomed to the goblins fighting for them, but Eric saw them as soldiers who could help, not helpless. They were a peaceful people, but even men of peace had to take up weapons and fight to maintain that peace.

They'd forgotten that and had been reminded earlier that day. Trey had been shot by an outsider, a member of the Meiji. It didn't matter who had decided the sanctuary was a target, they would soon regret it.

All was ready on his end. Some stood outside of the veil where Trey and his cousin Kindling had been attacked. Others remained near the temple as a solid force prepared for those stupid enough to try for the sacred edifice.

His mate had been right after all. Dimitri believed the forces against them were not acting alone, that an ancient enemy had been motivating this attack as part of its agenda. Komei Incorporated, the development company they had been fighting through legal means, had hidden their parent company from scrutiny. They'd underestimated Calyx, though, who'd done his research and discovered the Meiji involvement.

Dimitri's anger was palpable. "Calyx will fight in the human place of the law, but we will take this fight to the air. You, my love, will prepare to fight on land. It is my hope this will not be a necessity, but you have taught me to trust you, to trust your strength. Let us pray it is only guns we face. Anything more, and my father will have to ask the elders to use their magic."

"We'll do what we can, Dimitri. With the added force on the ground and you in the air, we should be able to defend the sanctuary. Now, come here and kiss me before you take off."

Dimitri laughed and took him into his arms.

Eric accepted his mate's kiss, licking the fangs that fell below his bottom lip. "We'll have to make use of that tongue of yours later." He winked and squeezed his husband's ass before letting him go.

"This is a promise, my love," Dimitri said before he opened his wings and shot up into the clouds.

Dimitri trusted him, trusted his strength, and respected him as a soldier. It was a gift hard won. When they had first met, his mate thought him less because he had one leg rather than two. They'd nearly lost their chance to have the greatest happiness the two of them had ever known because of his mate's stupidity — arrogant, stubborn, mired in the past. It had taken time, patience, and Eric's cane to show his mate the error of his ways.

Eric now stood waiting for the battle that would come, his troops dependent on his word while the man he loved more than life itself prepared to fight from above. When men came pouring out of the trees, he was ready.

It was unfortunate this had happened, but Haru and the elders felt the Meiji had chosen the time of the Autumn Feast thinking the Shugenja would be preparing for the celebration and lax in their security. They were wrong.

Eric hefted the automatic rifle on his shoulder. "Now," he bellowed. The sights and sound of his men running to face the enemy were the most amazing he'd ever witnessed. They were ready, and so was he.

Eric's aim was true as he picked off the humans running toward them, but that didn't mean the direction of their bullets was flawless. There were screams and shouts of pain on both sides. He looked up to see his goblin mate swooping down, dragging men off left and right, his eyes wild with fury. Eric's dick was hard as steel as he watched his mate fight.

Now is not the time for such thoughts.

But when this was over, he was fucking his Goblin, because Dimitri needed to be held down, to be worshipped, to be stripped of all his layers of responsibility, and to be loved. Eric was the man to do that.

Dimitri flew overhead searching for his mate, thankful when he spotted his bright red hair as he stood, men surrounding him, heeding his orders.

Mine. Eric was his other half, the love of his life, and he would challenge the sun every day for the blessing of calling him his own. He'd been a fool when they first met, but no longer. Eric had mastered him in body and soul, and Dimitri was his most honored disciple.

Focusing on the fight, he called his guards to him, and they attacked.

He enjoyed the rush of battle, the flow of power as he killed and maimed. It was his right to protect his people, and his goblin enjoyed every moment. He roared as he tore heads from bodies and ripped arms off torsos. He was covered in the blood of the enemy, as were his men. It was why they lived, to protect the sanctuary. It was the role he lusted for, but not as much as he yearned for the feel of Eric's cock between his thighs, his reward when this was done.

As the battle continued, Dimitri turned to see Calyx and Trey fighting together. He called to Calyx, happy to see his brother had joined the fray. His attention on Calyx, he missed seeing the bullet that tore through his wings, causing him to fall to the earth like Icarus before the sun.

When he opened his eyes, he found himself in his and Eric's home, his mate's face dirty and smeared but smiling endearingly.

"What has happened, my love?" Dimitri questioned.

"What needed to happen, my goblin. We won."

"We did?"

"Yes, even though the mightiest goblin of all fell from the sky, we did. You'd be proud of the way Calyx took your place and fought, his mate running as a wolf beneath him." Eric kissed him.

Dimitri savored his mate's flavor for a moment. "I am. I've never doubted my brother in his ability to fight. I trained him, after all."

Eric laughed, and his smile was the light to Dimitri's darkness.

"I'm also proud of you, my husband. I feel honored every day knowing you are mine in every way possible," Dimitri said. Years ago, he'd gone in search for a mate and came back with a man who challenged him, who made him better. He would be forever thankful for that during this Autumn Feast, and many more to come.

Dimitri turned at the sound of a weighty sigh to see a worn Trey held tightly in Calyx's arms.

"Something to say, Trey?" he asked.

"Not to you, but yes," Trey said. "Calyx?"

"Yes, my love."

"Let's go home."

Dimitri watched as the two left and turned back to his mate.

"What happened to the dead?"

"The earth opened and swallowed the bodies."

Dimitri nodded. *Good.*

No need to worry about that, especially since he'd rather focus on the man he loved.

"Eric?"

"Yes."

"Where's your cane?"

Eric's laugh was wicked, and Dimitri loved that, too.

CHAPTER SIX: SHUT UP, YOU FOOL

Trey sat with Calyx's arms around him, the sun waning in the sky, all evidence of the earlier skirmish swallowed by the earth.

Soon they would celebrate the Autumn Feast. There would be food, music, and dancing. Prayers would be said, and each person present would share their hopes and dreams, the reasons why they offered thanks. He knew many would be thankful for the goblins, for the elders, but Trey would be grateful for finding love, a home. He'd never had one before.

He'd seen Kindling once since the battle, walking with Haru, their gazes for each other alone. It would seem his cousin had a reason to be thankful, too.

"Calyx . . ." Trey began, turning in his lover's arms and kissing him gently on the neck.

"You don't have to say anything. I heard what Dimitri said, and it doesn't have to apply to us. I already know how blessed I am."

"Calyx —" Trey tried again.

"We don't even need to speak of marriage anymore. We're mates, and that's all that matters. It's enough. It will be enough. As long as I have you, that's enough."

"Calyx, my beautiful mate. Shut up."

Calyx sighed.

"I want you to listen. Just listen, okay?" Trey drew his mate's right hand to his mouth and kissed it tenderly. "My mother made me afraid to love. Afraid if I gave myself to someone, they would abuse that gift and destroy me in the

228

process. She was my mother. She had to be right, you know? So, when she told me not to release my wolf, no one would want me, and I would always be in danger, I believed that. I lived my life, afraid.

"Then you came, and I realized I could be loved. You love me, and that's the greatest gift I've ever known. So, it was hard, but I accepted that. But I still held myself back, kept myself away from giving all of me. You asked me to marry you, and it scared the shit out of me. Still does."

"Baby —" Calyx murmured.

"Shut up, Calyx. I'm still talking, and while I can't hold you in contempt, I can walk away."

Calyx sighed again.

"But I don't want to. I want this, what we have, to grow. And I want it forever, Calyx. Seeing Dimitri fall from the sky and watching Eric as he stood helpless, unable to do anything, I realized life is too short for me not to take all I can get and hold on. Hell, I could have died, and then, what? Miss the chance to enjoy everything I could have with the man I love? If only for one day. Five years. Twenty. I want every moment I can have, and I want that with you. I don't want to live life, wondering, and wishing. I want to grab it and hold on with all I can. I want it all, including your name."

Calyx took a deep breath. "Gods, Trey. I'd be happy to take yours. To take anything you're willing to give."

"Well, I'm not, Calyx. I want it all. I want you, a fresh start, to leave old ghosts behind. For me, marrying you, legalizing it according to human law, will make that happen, because I'm not just yours in the world of goblin and wolf, but yours for the entire world to see. That's what I want. Will you, Calyx Akiyama, give that to me? Will you marry me tomorrow during the Autumn Feast?"

Calyx's eyes were wet, but he laughed. "Well. Let me think. There's so much to consider."

Epilogue: New Beginnings

Haru stepped aside and presented his son to the man who had finally said *yes*. The day was beautiful, the moon bright in the sky and the spirits of his people celebratory. A perfect day for a wedding.

The elders began the festivities with prayers for the Autumn Feast. Mooncake was shared as stories were told. There were hugs and joy for all. The men of the sanctuary held their heads higher as their family praised them for defending the temple. There had been losses, and the survivors remembered each of the ones they lost, but they were together with much to be thankful for.

Before the meal, the time all had wished for arrived. Calyx and Trey knelt at the foot of the temple preparing to wed. After sharing a slice of mooncake, they stood and spoke their vows while Haru and his people looked on. His heart filled with joy as Calyx spoke the words he'd prayed to share with his mate for years now.

"I pledge to you my soul to keep for a lifetime to come. I bestow to you my name to shoulder as we make our path in this world."

"My name, not yours." Trey corrected.

Calyx's laugh was warm as he bent to kiss his mate on the cheek wiping away the tear that had settled there with shaking fingers.

"Correction. Forgive me, my love. I take your name to keep, to shoulder as we make our path in this world."

Trey nodded, his eyes bright with happiness.

The two had practiced the words that had been spoken for generations, but Haru knew his son wouldn't hesitate to grant Trey this concession, to give Trey the power he needed in their mating, and to show the man he loved that he was willing to submit to him as well. The tradition was for the stronger to bestow their name to the lesser.

Well, Trey is not Calyx's lesser. He is his equal, master of my son's heart.

As if the moon was pleased, its iridescent light brightened, touching all the Autumn Feast participants. There were sighs and gasps as her blessings were given to all.

A Tengu goblin had found his mate—a gift rarely discovered. Haru had never had his own. *Until now?* He had to wonder as he looked at the man standing next to him.

Haru smiled when Trey spoke his vows, adjusted to suit the mating of two unique individuals with their own way to love.

"I am honored to keep your soul as you keep mine, to bestow unto you my name, to stand guard and protect you for our lifetime. May our flame never extinguish so we blaze like the sun together forever, sheltering those in our keeping."

Haru startled when Kindling linked arms with him and smiled at him suggestively. He shook his head at the little imp, but when he tried to move, Kindling wouldn't let him go. The man was a lot stronger than anyone gave him credit for. He had no idea what to do with the sly wolf attached to his side, who only burrowed himself in further.

"Forever," Kindling murmured while Calyx and Trey finished their vows. He gripped Haru tighter when Calyx and Trey kissed, then drew his hand along Haru's back as Calyx and Trey signed the documents pronouncing them as husbands.

Haru shivered when Kindling whispered, "Next Autumn Feast be ready, Haru Akiyama. Of course, I might not be able to wait that long."

Perhaps Kindling would fit as Trey had already. Trey had accepted the responsibility of the sanctuary and its people, had promised to protect them alongside his mate.

Haru had been there when Calyx had challenged the sun, his sacrifice to the mating bond. His son flew proudly as he stretched out his wings, the sun's glorious rays behind him, casting his mate in his shadow down below.

And Trey had stood watching, waiting until Calyx had circled enough times to satisfy his need to show his mate he held no fear, that no matter what they faced, he would keep Trey safe.

When Calyx had fallen exhausted to the ground, Trey had been there to kiss his brow, to enfold him within his waiting arms, the two of them smiling, Calyx's expression grateful and Trey's hopeful.

The newest addition to their family had not believed Calyx would change his world to give Trey what he required. He'd questioned their bond and what he wanted of it. He'd been fearful and hesitant.

Now, he appeared a different man who celebrated the union he and Calyx shared. He'd found his place and accepted his role as a giver of knowledge to the young of the sanctuary, educating them and finding the necessary resources to ensure their health both physically and mentally.

Trey had blossomed, and after the battle, he'd approach Haru and asked him for Calyx's hand in marriage.

Too stunned to give the young man any grief, Haru had clasped the boy tightly to himself and kissed him on the forehead. His *yes* had been laden with emotion because he knew how very far Trey and Calyx had come. To finally have Calyx's dream made real was a prayer answered for Haru as well.

And now, as the two stood before them all, pronounced not only as mates but as husbands, Haru glowed within, his happiness for them both making his wings unfurl as if he would take flight and challenge the sun himself.

Would Calyx have changed his vows, his whole world to have his mate?

Of that, Haru had no doubt.

Would he do whatever was necessary to ensure his mate knew he was loved?

Well, that was what mates did when they said yes.

ABOUT THE DEJA BLACK

Deja Black had fantasies of men loving men, men who felt strongly, loved hard, and needed a hero. Then one great day she came across a book and discovered the world of m/m writing, encountered others who shared her obsession as much as she did, and found a world where she could not only be accepted for the lives and loves she envisioned, but she could create them too. So why not? Why not take the stories she would write and throw away as a teenager, grow them, dream them, and make them a reality where she could let them live their story, and make them real for someone else? And she did. Now, with the support of her hubby and some intense time management, she is learning to balance her family of two energetic children at home along with the many students she teaches every day as well as her passion of writing what she loves to read.

Deja is always interested in connecting to new people who also share her love, so please feel free to contact her at:

Facebook: www.facebook.com/deja.black.69

Blog: dejablack77.blogspot.com

Twitter: @DejaBlack69